Praise for *Life, Bra*

"This novel by the acclaimed Maraini weaves together the c distinct voices of a daughter, who live together in contemporary Rome. Elvira Di Fabio's translation captures the rhythm, style, and pace of each woman's voice beautifully. A fast and entertaining read!"

> —Tommasina Gabriele, author of *Dacia Maraini's Narratives of Survival: (Re)Constructed*

"Brilliantly translated by Elvira Di Fabio, and eloquently introduced by Sara Teardo, *Life, Brazen and Garish: A Tale of Three Women* is a riveting medley of epistolary and diaristic women's voices. Dacia Maraini's polyphonic narrative mesmerizes and implicates us in its woman-centered family drama. The quotidian explodes—and we run for cover."

> —Edvige Giunta, coeditor of *Talking to the Girls: Intimate and Political Essays on the Triangle Shirtwaist Factory Fire*

"*Life, Brazen and Garish* will mesmerize and completely absorb the English-speaking reader regardless of their familiarity with Dacia Maraini's work. Maraini shapes this story of three women connected by intergenerational family ties (*nonna*, mother, and daughter) by exploring their distinct ways of expressing themselves. Elvira di Fabio's skillful and insightful translation of *Tre donne. Una storia d'amore e disamore* is a vibrant example of the power of words to shape identities."

> —Irene Zanini-Cordi, coauthor of *Courting Celebrity: The Autobiographies of Angela Veronese and Teresa Bandettini*

Life, Brazen and Garish

Other Voices of Italy

Series Editors: Alessandro Vettori, Sandra Waters, and Eilis Kierans

This series presents texts in a variety of genres originally written in Italian. Much like the symbiotic relationship between the wolf and the raven, its principal aim is to introduce new or past authors—who have until now been marginalized—to an English-speaking readership. This series also highlights contemporary transnational authors, as well as writers who have never been translated or who are in need of a fresh/contemporary translation. The series further aims to increase the appreciation of translation as an art form that enhances the importance of cultural diversity.

Life, Brazen and Garish: A Tale of Three Women, penned by one of Italy's most celebrated authors, brings fresh perspective to this series through its focus on the power of translation to bridge different people and cultures. The plot follows the interweaving stories of three generations of women—a grandmother, mother, daughter—who for financial reasons live in the same home and communicate their woes in stylistically different forms. Gesuina, a stage actress in her heyday, is a sharp and theatrical prima donna who savors the sound of her own voice and expresses herself via audio recordings. Her daughter, Maria, on the other hand, is a musing romantic and translator who pens eloquent letters in which she mulls over, or rather translates, the behavior of her mother and daughter. Lori, the youngest of the women, is an impetuous teenager who moves a million miles an hour, as reflected in the racing thoughts she pens in her diary. It is, however, only after Maria suffers a tragic accident that her mother and daughter are moved to speak one another's language. And so, as their situations and relations evolve, the women's unique voices blend together—not unlike the voices of author and translator. By the end of the book, the reader is left poignantly aware of the multiple voices rooted deep inside all of us.

Life, Brazen and Garish

~

A Tale of Three Women

DACIA MARAINI

Translated by Elvira G. Di Fabio

Foreword by Sara Teardo

Rutgers University Press

New Brunswick, Camden, and Newark, New Jersey

London and Oxford

Rutgers University Press is a department of Rutgers, The State University of New Jersey, one of the leading public research universities in the nation. By publishing worldwide, it furthers the University's mission of dedication to excellence in teaching, scholarship, research, and clinical care.

Library of Congress Cataloging-in-Publication Data
Names: Maraini, Dacia, author. | Di Fabio, Elvira G., translator. | Teardo, Sara, writer of foreword.
Title: Life, brazen and garish : a tale of three women / Dacia Maraini ; translated by Elvira G. Di Fabio ; foreword by Sara Teardo.
Other titles: Tre donne. English
Description: New Brunswick : Rutgers University Press, 2024. | Series: Other voices of Italy | Translation of Tre donne. Una storia d'amore e disamore. Rizzoli, 2017. | Includes bibliographical references.
Identifiers: LCCN 2023026190 | ISBN 9781978839731 (paperback) | ISBN 9781978839748 (hardcover) | ISBN 9781978839755 (epub) | ISBN 9781978839762 (pdf)
Subjects: LCGFT: Domestic fiction. | Novels.
Classification: LCC PQ4873.A69 T7413 2024 | DDC 853/.914—dc23/eng/20230609
LC record available at https://lccn.loc.gov/2023026190

A British Cataloging-in-Publication record for this book is available from the British Library

© 2017 Rizzoli Libri S.p.A./Rizzoli, Milano, Italy

© 2018 Mondadori Libri S.p.A., originally published by Rizzoli BUR, Milano, Italy
Translation of Tre donne. Una storia d'amore e disamore. Rizzoli, 2017.
Translation by Elvira G. Di Fabio © 2024

References to internet websites (URLs) were accurate at the time of writing. Neither the author nor Rutgers University Press is responsible for URLs that may have expired or changed since the manuscript was prepared.

rutgersuniversitypress.org

Contents

Foreword

The Power of Words: Three Women's Quest for Meaning and Self-Discovery

One of the most popular Italian contemporary authors, Dacia Maraini is a writer of many talents. A novelist, playwright, poet, journalist, and activist, she published her first novel in 1962, at twenty-six, and has never stopped since, winning major national and international literary awards. Her most famous novels, *Bagheria*, *Isolina*, and the worldwide bestseller *La lunga vita di Marianna Ucrìa* (The Silent Duchess), have all been translated into English. And now, thanks to the newly launched series Other Voices of Italy (OVOI) by Rutgers University Press, the English-speaking public can discover two more recent works and gain a wider grasp of her long-standing interests and experimentation with different writing styles. After her *Chiara di Assisi. Elogio della disobbedienza* (2013), translated by Jane Tylus as *In Praise of Disobedience: Clare of Assisi, a Novel*, prefaced by Rudolph Bell, OVOI is publishing *Tre donne. Una storia d'amore e disamore* (2017), in this excellent rendition by Elvira G. Di Fabio, who, echoing a poem by Baudelaire that plays a key role in the narrative, has carved out the apt title *Life, Brazen and Garish: A Tale of Three Women.* To fully appreciate the complexity and thematic richness of this novel, it is necessary to position it not only within the precise historical and cultural context in which Maraini lived but also within an intricate network of interconnections among her various works, which have consistently been characterized by a strong intratextual coherence.

Maraini's life has been marked by battles fought with courage and determination against patriarchal hegemony and oppression. Born in 1936 in Florence to Topazia Alliata, a Sicilian aristocrat and artist, and Fosco Maraini, an adventurous ethnologist and travel writer, she moved to Japan in 1938, where her father was to conduct research. Her life was tragically scarred when her parents refused to give their allegiance to the new Repubblica di Salò, the new fascist government established by Benito Mussolini in the north of Italy after the country, formerly part of the Tripartite Pact with Germany and Japan, signed the armistice with the Allies during World War II. The whole family, including Dacia's two younger sisters, was interned in a concentration camp between 1943 and 1945—a traumatic experience she would later recall in her 1993 lyrical memoir *Bagheria* and in *La nave per Kobe*, a 2001 novel based on her mother's diaries. Back in Italy, she studied in Palermo, and after her parents' separation, she moved to Rome at nineteen, to live with her father. She quickly became involved with the dynamic literary world of the capital, collaborating on journals, publishing short stories, poems, and articles, and actively participating in the lively theater scene. She eventually founded and directed an all-female theater collective called Teatro della Maddalena, whose unwavering focus was to expose the (unwritten) history of women's oppression throughout the centuries. Her involvement in issues such as abortion, divorce, and abuse led her to endorse the battles of the Italian feminist movement, which in the 1970s fiercely confronted the male-controlled structure of power and society and advocated for sexual liberation.

Her work, which encompasses poetry collections, novels, plays (more than thirty), movie scripts, and essays, progressively reflected her broader social and historical perspectives. After her first volume *La vacanza* (The Vacation, 1962), a controversial story of a girl discovering her sexuality in a male world, she pursued her urge to break roles and traditions tied to a misogynistic past by denouncing a wider system of suppression of female voices, especially with her novels *Isolina* (1985) and *The Silent Duchess* (1990). The latter, widely regarded as her masterpiece and translated into almost thirty languages, focuses on the life of a deaf-mute duchess living in Sicily in the eighteenth century, forced at age thirteen to marry her uncle, also her abuser. With *Voci* (Voices, 1994), Maraini experimented with the noir genre to confront the hotly debated topic of *femminicidio*, the killing of women and girls by intimate partners or family members, whereas in the collection of short stories *Buio* (Darkness, 1999), inspired by real-life events and awarded Italy's most prestigious literary prize, the Premio Strega, she courageously addressed violence against minors. With her *In Praise of Disobedience*, Maraini resumed investigating women in history, offering a portrait of Chiara of Assisi, an exemplary religious figure from the thirteenth century, whom she considered a symbol of independence and free will for her early rebellion against her noble family and the constraints of medieval society.

Like Chiara, the author herself has inspired generations of readers and writers. She travels internationally to give lectures and seminars and occasionally teaches as a visiting professor at prestigious universities such as Harvard and the

Zurich Polytechnic. Among her latest publications, it is worth mentioning *Caro Pier Paolo* (2022), a collection of imagined letters addressed to the late Pier Paolo Pasolini, one of Italy's leading intellectuals of the twentieth century and a close friend of Maraini.

Many of the provocative, gender-related themes and social issues mentioned above are deftly intertwined in *Life, Brazen and Garish: A Tale of Three Women*. In the novel, three generations of women—Gesuina, the grandmother, her widowed daughter, Maria, and her granddaughter, Lori—live under the same roof in a complicated and fragile equilibrium. They put up with one another "out of necessity," yet they are extremely close and intimate. The original title, *Tre donne. Una storia d'amore e disamore* (Three women. A story of love and disaffection), draws our attention to the theme of love and its lack thereof, but this novel is also, above all, a testimony to the powerful impact of language and writing.

The story of *Three Women* unfolds, alternating the voices of the three characters through different narrative strategies, in a typical Maraini fashion, placing women as both speaking subjects and observers: the daughter writes a diary, the mother crafts elegant letters to her distant partner, and the grandmother records her voice in a portable tape recorder, keeping "an oral diary of sorts," transcribed on the page. The passion for writing runs in their family (as it did in Maraini's); as Lori puts it, it is a sort of "family disease" passed down from one generation to the next. The narrative spans a bit more than a year; it is an eventful period during which the trio and their daily lives are turned upside down by unexpected changes. Maria's longtime partner, François, who lives in Lille, France, finally decides to come to Rome to spend Christmas with his lover and her family. Perfectly fluent in Italian and passionate about poetry, the handsome and well-mannered François appears like an angel, "resplendent like a Saint Michael ready to pierce the dragon" (41), to the eyes of Lori and Gesuina, who both admire and secretly covet the fascinating gentleman. Unlike the prude Maria, who blindly believes in pure, romantic love, the sixty-year-old grandmother and her teenage granddaughter are not shy of exploring the needs of desire: while the disinhibited Gesuina regularly exchanges passionate kisses with a young baker in the back of his store (sublimating any erotic drive), the rebellious Lori has found a sexual partner in a boy her age. François's visit triggers a series of dramatic consequences that shatter the lives of the three protagonists, forcing them to adapt to a new reality through a drastic transformation evoked, in the text, by the symbolic image of a larva turning into a butterfly.

Reflecting Maraini's penchant for inter- and intratextual connections in her oeuvre, *Life, Brazen and Garish* revisits an older play titled *Mela* that Maraini wrote and successfully toured in several Italian cities in 1982 with her theater collective. *Mela* is a two-act comedy in which a mother, her daughter, and her grandmother exchange ironic remarks and rebukes in their kitchen. The main thematic aspect of the novel comes from the play: three generations of women, with contrasting personalities, barely contained within the walls of a house, whose unity is threatened by an unsettling turn of events. The mother's counterpart in the play, Rosaria, loyal and principled, sacrifices herself to provide for the other two, who are happily "free" from responsibilities—if the mother is the proverbial ant, the other two are grasshoppers. But Rosaria is also a *sessantottina*, deeply connected to the social and political issues of the 1960s; she is politically involved and defends left-wing uprisings, proudly singing their anthem, the *Internationale*. Following many of her comrades' destinies, and lost in her revolutionary dreams, Rosaria is bound to be a victim, but the potentially tragic ending of the play is comically averted thanks to a workers' strike. This political dimension is completely erased in the novel. Furthermore, in the narrative, Maraini adds depth and complexity to plot and characters and opts for a different resolution, taking the chance to elaborate on pressing social and ethical issues currently under debate in our modern world, such as abortion and end-of-life decisions. She also introduces the male characters, completely offstage in *Mela*, only to critique their ineptitude, fickleness, and latent attachment to the vestiges of patriarchal society.

The play's conversation is witty and fast paced, and the dialogic exchange is enriched and complicated by the fact that the three women's trains of thought seem at times to overlap and intersect, each resonating with one another. It is precisely this textual aspect—the juxtaposition and alternation of the women's words and reflections—that is placed in the foreground of *Life, Brazen and Garish*, thus shaping the structure of the novel. Alternating voices is a common characteristic of Maraini's work that has been perfected over the years through her experimentation with different writing strategies. For instance, the author has explored the self-creation of a female voice through the epistolary form as a way to elicit empathy and identification from readers in her 1981 *Lettere a Marina*, *Dolce per sè* (1997) and in the more recent *Trio* (2020). In *Praise of Disobedience*, she combined both letters with diary entries, another form of writing commonly associated with women and their development of self-awareness. The diary, indeed, was typically employed in the 1970s by politically engaged literature, and it is present, for example, in Maraini's 1997 feminist manifesto, *Woman at War*. Both forms—epistolary writing and journaling—are effective vehicles to help readers directly access the analytical process of the protagonists' minds, generating an intimate connection between the reader and the first-person narrators.

All these textual strategies have been relevant in the making of our novel. In *Life, Brazen and Garish*, letters, diary entries, and voice recordings are devices that, while advancing the plot, unveil how the protagonists' relationships evolve over time and how their thoughts and feelings undergo subtle but revelatory changes, bringing them closer together by the end of the novel. All three female figures are deeply invested in trying to make sense of themselves and the world around them, developing different interpretations based on their outlooks on reality, as reflected in their writings. Reading Lori's diary, for example, we witness a progressive coming to terms with her own restlessness and impulsivity, a state that mirrors her inability to pause and reflect. Her gradual awareness of herself and her surroundings stems from a sort of understanding by free association; her mental correspondences do not rely on a rational process but on trusting her own feelings and intuitions. For example, talking about a secret she "doesn't wanna share," she claims that "the secret will remain secret because that's what my body wants, a body that lives on unknown impulses and happy departures and joys conquered without even knowing it." This prerational, intuitive knowing that is transposed in her free-associative writing helps her navigate the chaotic reality and any unexpected turns of fate.

Maria is also engaged in a process of self-awareness through the power of words. In her case, she uses writing to investigate and anxiously question the fragility and ephemerality of the human condition, thus reflecting her own frailty as a learned woman enclosed in a detached, literary dimension, where "recollections of literary passages . . . intertwine with lived moments" as if she had experienced them herself. Hence Maria's homage to *lentezza*, in contrast to modern-life hectic rhythms, a slowness that allows her to transpose and seed ideas onto the page, and her opting for the old-fashioned epistolary genre against the dehumanizing effects of technology. Slowness is commended for its "hidden but profound value: the slowness of thought, the slowness of the word, the slowness of writing"; only a slow-paced and selective process allows thought to come to full fruition because it "plants its seeds in the flesh, stretches out its roots, grows, turns into a leaf, flower, tree, the breath of the universe." Her ideas gradually become embodied on the page, acquiring consistency and form.

For the free-spirited grandmother, instead, reality itself in all its manifestations and forms holds a hidden truth that calls for interpretation. A tattoo written on the body tells a tale; it is a "dream on the flesh" that can be read and brought to life, whereas a derriere with its constellation of moles and imperfections can "speak." Gesuina, a former actress who is now earning a living by giving injections, claims she can perfectly understand that language in her characteristically nonedulcorated style: "I concentrate on the geography of moles at the bottom of a back, and I see them as constellations. . . . I have fun making those asses talk." Thus, whereas Lori perceives reality through associations and Maria through literary filters, Gesuina relates to her surroundings through the revelatory language of bodies.

By foregrounding the power of words, Maraini draws our attention to both the overt and latent meanings of the textual fabric and offers insights into the multilayered structure that informs not only the narrative but the semantic level as well. She uncovers the multiple strata of signification embedded within words both directly, through the use of etymologies and *nomi parlanti*, "talking names" (e.g., Gesuina, which is female for Jesus, or Cascadei, which will be later discussed), and indirectly, through the passionate plea of the grandmother in support of the use of "raw" words and her rejection of euphemisms ("pretentious ways to camouflage reality, mask it and make it more pleasant," as Maraini wrote in her 1987 essay "Reflections on the Logical and Illogical Bodies of My Sexual Compatriots"). For the grandmother (and for the author), "lewd words," like *culo* (ass), are irreplaceable in their nakedness; their "polite" synonyms would only be too "overdressed" and would manipulate the readers' imaginations while simply preserving the status quo. Gesuina proudly asserts, "Let's just say that an ass is an ass and there's nothing wrong with pronouncing that word, even children hear it willingly." Echoing Gesuina, Maraini also points out in that same essay how (patriarchal) society does not accept the use of obscene and "ugly" words, particularly from women, because it spoils their image as immaculate and obedient subjects. Obscenity betrays a crude and "unpurged" vision of the world that women cannot afford to have: "female writing meant or used to mean something sentimental, delicate, imprecise, crepuscular."[1]

Every word contains a world in itself, a story, that can be traced down through its origins: the word *caffè* (coffee), for example, is charged with its past because, as Gesuina explains, "it comes from the word *qahwa*, which the Turks then transformed into *kahve*, which finally became coffee for us"; Maria, in contrast, comments that "the name tulip . . . comes from the Turkish 'tullband,'" which means "turban" and poignantly observes that underneath the simple name of a delicate and colorful flower that has become the popular symbol of a Nordic country emerges a different story, "an Orient that faces the south."

Words are spellbinding thanks to their wide spectrum of signification and unique combinations of meaning and sound; they even transmit sensual pleasure because "something in the sound of the words can get through to [our] brains, passing as steamy water" even through closed ears. They can awaken the body and its senses: as Gesuina claims, "words can be sensual, just like kisses" and the words of her new lover Filippo, whom she met online, "weigh in with a subtle and intense pleasure. . . . It's a lively emotion that slithers up my spine."

Can such a multilayered semantic wealth be transferred into another language? The difficult task of translation is one of the themes of the novel. Maria is a translator by profession, now in the final stages of completing her rendition of Gustave Flaubert's masterpiece *Madame Bovary*.[2] Portrayed as constantly "keeping up with the words," Maria—herself very close to Madame Bovary in her inability to cope with reality—knows all too well that words are unique and almost irreplaceable and sadly notes, "it is a shame that in Italian the sounds of the words are lost, words that for a perfectionist like Flaubert have a precise meaning, almost carnal I would say" (4). Let us pause on the adjective "carnal" (fleshy, sensual) for a moment. Maria's final version, born out of her hard work, is presented like a delivery: when the book arrives, it is delicately placed in her arms, and here the English translation of Gesuina's comment provides a clue: "Here's the book that you *labored* over, Maria" (emphasis added). For Maraini, in fact, the very act of translating, as stated in a 1996 introduction to her rendition of Joseph Conrad's *The Secret Sharer*, "with its physical gesture of leaning over the page for a long time, with emotion, not ignoring even a tiny secret of the text . . . has above all maternal characteristics."

Can the labor of translation do justice to the force and impact of the original text? When the literary, poetic discourse retains its powerful combination of "music and thought," Maraini claims, it still conveys its extraordinary effects and could even turn, like the original, into an instrument of salvation. It is Maria who provides a key example of the formidable power of the written word when she recalls a book of memoirs written by a Holocaust survivor that she once translated. Some prisoners in a concentration camp, gathering in the disgusting latrines after a dreary day of toil, would secretly recite poems they had memorized in their youth in a "soft chant" and a "rhythmic hum." In those dreadful conditions, "the poems would miraculously give them the strength to go on, . . . the strength to survive in that place of torture and death," not unlike what Primo Levi experienced in *If This Is a Man* (Survival in Auschwitz) when reciting Dante's Ulysses canto. It was that moving testimony that helped Maria learn "the kind of power that words can have when they become music and thought, a poignant and moving strategy of survival." The conclusion of *Life, Brazen and Garish* confirms the healing, therapeutic power of words that not only nurtures our imaginations and dreams but can help us cope with trauma and soothe our suffering. A couple of verses from Baudelaire's *Les fleurs du mal*, recited twice, at key moments in the narrative, proves this point. These verses, taken from the poem "La fin de la journée" (End of the Day), contrast life, in its impudence and raucousness, to the replenishing, soothing darkness of the night-death and reveal the chaotic, irrational movement of human existence. It is François, Maria's French lover, who recites them for the first time in their original language: "Sous une lumière blafarde / Court, danse et se tord sans raison / La Vie, impudente et criarde." But these same verses reemerge in translation at the very end of the novel, unleashing all their revelatory, regenerating force and thus marking the denouement of the story:

"Under a dim light / Runs, dances and twists for no reason / Life, brazen and garish." Baudelaire's powerful, poetic words are indeed, as the reader will ascertain, an instrument of salvation.

The act of translation entails acceptance and recognition of the other's discourse. It opposes, as such, any attitude of appropriation and possession of the voice of the other—what the androcentric discourse has been doing over the centuries, according to Maraini the feminist activist, manipulating, internalizing, and silencing women's voices. This patriarchal strategy is explicitly denounced in the book by Gesuina and Lori. The grandmother laments the jealousy and possessiveness of her new lover Filippo who wants to control her "almost as if I were his property" because men are used to "appropriating women's bodies as they please. Bodies that when they grow distant and show reluctance and independence arouse their anger, jealousy, their resolve to possess and dominate." In her fierce attack, Gesuina echoes the author's long battles for equal rights against the historical privileges of men; the grandmother, in fact, could not pursue her desire to study medicine because of her family's opposition. Confined to a male-dominated perspective, women seem to be destined to sacrifice; Maria, for example, works tirelessly to provide her man all he wants and "will soon grow a halo and even wings, but she will never fly away, because she's a housewife," as her daughter Lori dryly remarks. Contrary to Maria, though, Gesuina refuses the role of the selfless grandmother, willing to make sacrifices because, as she claims, she is "a free person and not a family institution." Even if her freedom will have to be negotiated with new responsibilities later in the story, constrained roles and historical privileges must nonetheless be brought to light and denounced in their persistence.

The effort to lay bare the web of biases and obligations entrapping women seems to belong to the family's destiny, as their last name, Cascadei, aptly reveals. The three women aim at dethroning (hinted at by the verb *cascare* [to fall]) the *dei* (gods) off their pedestal to unveil what lies beneath the privilege of (male) deities while creating their own mythology. Gods, the heavenly powers, are "vengeful tyrants" who want humankind "to remain submissive and obedient." A divine figure that must be demystified and dethroned is, for example, François, who is depicted at first as "the god of love" and "a new Hermes with wings on his ankles"; even a man like him, educated and sensitive, ends up gradually imposing his lifestyle on the women. Nevertheless, his character is progressively uncovered in his untrustworthiness and exposed in his incapacity to take accountability for his actions.

If the tyrannical gods must be challenged, Prometheus is the hero who can intervene to help.[3] A recurrent mention in the book, the Titan Prometheus is a demigod who helped humans defy Zeus's command and was harshly punished in retaliation. Lori draws a lengthy profile of him, recalling through her mom's words, how he was a friend of humankind, who stole from Athena and Zeus to give intelligence, memory, and fire to man, and bore the anger of the gods chained to a rock and subjected to eternal torture. The rebellious Prometheus embodies the heroic human will to challenge injustice and authority and to "steal fire from death and grasp onto life." In the novel, the mythical hero transcends the gendered discourse and moves beyond any constructed, fixed identity: Prometheus in fact is the name that Lori gives to her female dog, occasionally called Promethea by the other women. Prometheus, as a guiding light, deserves to be rescued from the gods' ire. Gesuina has a revelatory dream, a frequent literary device in Maraini's narrative, where she envisions a two-headed dog that in a human voice tells her to organize an expedition to the highest mountains to free the hero from the eagle. Prometheus in his disobedience against the rules of Zeus, the controlling father whom Maraini in her 1987 essay once defined as "a bearded and intolerant god to whom we [women] have promised devotion and obedience," represents a new mythology for women's rebellion against submission.

Provider of light and knowledge, the image of Prometheus can be metaphorically seen as a mediator, bringing us back to the theme of language and translation. In a parallel fashion, the figure of the translator acts as a mediator, building bridges and shedding light on the differences between languages and cultures. Regarding the challenges that Elvira G. Di Fabio had to face in her translation of this novel, I would like to offer the reader a few final considerations as a concluding note. As we have discussed before, the three women's personalities are mirrored in their peculiar linguistic register and means of communication. Lori, a disillusioned teenager, in search of her own identity within the tight-knit family group, proves her impulsivity and rejection of any conventions with her colloquial language, jotting down in her diary a discourse oblivious to punctuation rules and close to a stream-of-consciousness narration. Her entries, vivid and rich in animal metaphors, share a few traits with her "accomplice," *nonna* Gesuina, and her informal recordings. They both describe the mother in similar terms (*svampita* and *cieca* [airhead and blind]) and blame her for her backwardness and sentimentalism. Gesuina, in contrast, can be cruder in her expressions than her granddaughter and uses more profanities because they can better reflect, as we have seen, her point of view. Her language is as direct and simple as if she were talking to a friend, although her acting career sometimes seeps out through quotations from Carlo Goldoni or Luigi Pirandello. Gesuina deplores the intellectual and elegant language preferred by her daughter, Maria, a language filled with elaborate vocabulary and enriched by literary references. The precision of Maria's language mirrors the profound attention she pays to words out of her professional habit while, at the same time, it betrays her laboriously structured, and therefore fragile, vision of the world.

Elvira G. Di Fabio has done an exquisite job respecting the linguistic complexity of the original text while keeping it readable and comprehensible. She managed to direct and orient the reader even in relation to Lori's free, unrestrained speech. Thus, Lori's diary entries preserve the qualities of her fragmented, slangy discourse, with her rapid sequence of short sentences and the frantic and inchoate stream of thoughts. And yet Di Fabio, mindful of the overlapping of the women's vocabulary and the progressive mirroring of each other's style in their texts, knowingly allows the reader to be part of their tight community and perceive in their writing not only a moment of self-discovery but a relational space in which they can redefine and negotiate their subjectivities.

Sara Teardo
Princeton University

Notes

1. Maraini, "Reflections on the Logical and Illogical Bodies of My Sexual Compatriots," in *The Pleasure of Writing: Critical Essays on Dacia Maraini,* ed. Rodica Diaconescu-Blumenfeld and Ada Testaferri. Purdue University Press, 2000, p. 25.
2. It is worth noting that Maraini herself devoted to the famous novel a lengthy critical study, *Cercando Emma: Gustave Flaubert e*

la signora Bovary [Searching for Emma: Gustave Flaubert and Madame Bovary] in 1993.

3. Maraini once again draws our attention to the etymology of the Titan's name: "in Greek Prometheus means he who reflects first" before acting. Thinking about the consequences of one's actions means preventing possible regrets and future suffering, a lesson that Lori, in particular, will have to learn. In addition, considering that this mythical figure is also linked to the gift of foreseeing, at a second reading we can detect in the unfolding of the text a few foreboding statements that are ironically noticeable only in hindsight—adding, once again, another layer of interpretation over the literal meaning.

Translator's Note

When I first read Dacia Maraini's *Tre donne: Una storia d'amore e disamore*, I immediately knew I wanted to translate it into English. Certainly, as Carla Carotenuto (2022) states, the novel "adds a fundamental piece to the mosaic of her work,"[1] with themes ranging from intergenerational relationships, reality versus illusion, struggles over life and death, knowledge and ignorance, eros and agape, hate and happiness, love and disaffection (if only we had an equivalent of *disamore* in English!). At the same time, I found myself frequently chuckling, something I rarely do as a reader of Maraini's works, but Gesuina's unwittingly comic philosophizing invariably draws out such a reaction. Ultimately, however, the impetus behind my desire to translate this novel rests in her use of stylistics to define her three protagonists. Translation is magically revelatory. It gets you deeper into the text than even a careful reading would allow. The effect was not lost on me, and the choices I have made evolved from my understanding of Maraini's decision to utilize a style of writing, rather than description provided by the voice of the author or narrator, to define her protagonists.

The story chronicles a year in the life of three women, a grandmother, her daughter, and her granddaughter, all living together under one roof. We learn of their interactions and personalities only through each woman's stylistically varied form of recorded voices or thoughts: Lori's diary entries, Maria's letters, Gesuina's audio recordings. All three voices—that is, styles—reflect the essence of the characters, and as translator, I made conscious choices to reflect that essence.

Lori, the youngest of the three women, writes in her diary using the impetuous, spontaneous language of adolescence. The uninhibited teenager avoids facing conflicts by flying off on her moped, her life's speed represented by her written testimony with sporadic and misplaced punctuation, her adolescent confusion voiced in run-on sentences and unclear time frames. To my editors' annoyance, I insisted on preserving that stylistic choice precisely because it assists the reader in assessing Lori's character and state of mind. Even Gesuina recognizes this mirroring of her granddaughter's character: "If I were to address you with Lori's ramshackle and verbose words, not only would you not understand, but you would feel almost offended by the lack of air in the sentences" (July 22). Please, dear reader (and editors), do not be offended by my insistence on preserving Lori's breathlessness, but patiently read through her ramblings as if you were listening to the confused, foolhardy teenager that she is.

In addition to maintaining the lack of punctuation and verbosity, I consciously chose to further emphasize Lori's breathlessness by using contractions—that is, "doesn't" versus "does not" or "there's" instead of "there is." Although contractions occur regularly in English, they do not in Italian, and although they are part of natural oral speech, I chose to represent Lori's written discourse with the "lack of air" that such contractions imply. Even her name, as Gesuina notes, reflects abbreviation and speed: "And come to think of it, I don't understand why they gave her the name Loredana, to then just turn around and call her Lori" (December 21).

Maria (with whom I share a translation methodology of writing in notebooks and then transcribing to computer) uses the language of a romantic, a learned researcher, and most significantly, a translator who chooses words with an intention to bridge cultures, experiences, and generations. Contrary to her daughter's style, Maria's letters honor the beauty of the slowness she relishes: "Slowness has its own hidden but profound value: the slowness of thought, the slowness of the word, the slowness of writing, the great privilege in a time of careless swiftness; the slowness that plants its seeds in the flesh, stretches out its roots, grows, turns into a leaf, flower, tree, the breath of the universe" (November 23). Consequent to this deliberate slowness, she affirms that "life spreads out in front of us, it lengthens, it gloriously protracts" (December 17). And it is precisely because of this philosophy that I have chosen to protract Maria's phrasing where I have contracted Lori's. Maria, the pensive translator whose detailed observations are so concentrated on the slowness of the word that she does not see the circumstances that are unfolding around her, therefore expresses herself in sentences slowed down by expanded, uncontracted verb forms.

Gesuina, erstwhile stage actress turned unlicensed nurse, has a voice that is sensible, down to earth, and at the same time escapist. As vestige of her time in the theater, she orally records her thoughts and experiences, reciting to a ghost audience. Gesuina has lived the longest and has gone through the most changes. She adapts to whatever life throws at her. At this stage in her life, she is exercising her freedom, flirting with virtual and nonsexual love. She even admits to acting more like a daughter to Maria, one who needs to be taken care of, rather than a responsible older adult. At this pivotal moment in the novel, however, Gesuina (literally) steps out of the shoes of an irresponsible flirt and takes on the role of mother. "When Maria was alive and active, I considered myself more a daughter than a mother; now I have to be the mother to a daughter who is no longer my mother but hopelessly my daughter and dependent on me for every need of her inert body" (July 22). Not only is Gesuina reverting to the role of mother that her daughter, Maria, once assumed, but she recognizes a change in her way of thinking and expression that sounds like her daughter's: "But this is more like an argument that my daughter, Maria, would make, not so customary to my lips, out of character for me and my mental habits. Am I turning into her? Are my pressing years softening and fading me? Is Lori's pregnancy making me change my style?" (May 2). As she tries to reach her comatose daughter, she takes on a style that is familiar to Maria: "A somewhat literary prayer, I realize, my daughter, but it is precisely by resorting to the language that is familiar to you that I try to speak to you" (July 22). All this means that the reader will notice a stylistic change in Gesuina's recordings that is closer to Maria's letters. This is intentional on the part of the author, an intention that as translator I have honored. The two women grow closer, come to an understanding, merge through their language, their choice of phrase and imagery. In the end, Gesuina is the one who draws Maria out, by speaking to her not in the style of her own sensible language but in the adopted literary style that she knows her daughter will recognize and understand.

Through translation, I have come to the realization that these three distinct, generational voices are in fact representative of a life's journey. The three women often use the same words to describe situations they encounter, and as such, we recognize a stylistic epigenesis of each one in the other, Lori in Gesuina, Maria in Lori, Maria in Gesuina. Maria is a translator. So as translator, I found myself face-to-face with the profession and the responsibility not so much to interpret but to bridge. Maria's voice translates languages and cultures, and in terms of her place within the family, hers is a voice between generations and life experiences. As the novel evolves, Maria loses her voice, but it echoes in Gesuina. She is the reason Lori and Gesuina become a force for life and for the revival and transmission of life.

By extension to the reader, each of us has different voices within us, a Lori, a Maria, a Gesuina, voices that will evolve as our life experiences play out. This is a lesson, an awareness worth sharing with the world, hence my true desire to translate Maraini's novel: to spread the voice or as is said in Italian, *spargere la voce*.

Elvira G. Di Fabio

Note

1. C. Carotenuto, "Femminile e maschile in *Tre donne. Una storia d'amore e disamore* di Dacia Maraini," *Open Journal of Humanities* 10 (2022): 61–85.

Life, Brazen and Garish

November 23

I hate diaries but like a fool I have one in my hand and I'm writing in it too, the problem is where the hell to hide it, luckily my mom isn't nosy, but my grandmother is, a monkey that sticks her nose into everything, even if she would never turn me in, she's like me, but I don't feel like having her read what I write, it's private property, no entry, go away, shoo! I hammered a hole into the wall that is quite thick and then I closed up the hole with a steel sheet that runs up and down and can be opened and closed with an eyelet-headed lock and that's good enough for me, then I hung a picture over it and that's that, a habit I've had since I was child: a diary, with all these books and notebooks all around, my mom is always telling me: read! write! and with my little hands that could barely hold a pen upright, I tried to please her, scribbling, drawings, swirls, and a few words with the handwriting of a trained dog, a family disease, a wretched habit that infected me with a disease, after all there are family diseases, aren't there? here I am with my notebook in hand, like my grandmother and then my mom before me, even if my grandmother was a stage actress for many years and she doesn't like to write, but she does like to talk and so she records her thoughts on tape, an oral diary of sorts, my grandfather before he died apparently wrote poetry and he would encourage her to put her thoughts on paper, even my father, who died of leukemia when he was around thirty-eight years old, used to write, mostly sports articles, so my mom says, and I barely remember him because he died when I was three and my mother was all alone and had to find a job, and what could she do, since writing and reading in different languages for her was like breathing? a translator, of course! she couldn't do otherwise, she'd work and still works thirteen hours a day, she practically forgets to eat just to keep up with the words . . . the point is they pay her very little and she's always behind in her bills, it's a good thing my grandmother earns some money giving shots, she's so good at it everyone in the neighborhood knows her and they call her from all over the place.

Dear François,
Recently my daughter, Lori, asked me how it is possible we have been writing to each other for so many years. What would you have answered? It seems quite natural to me; it is our way of speaking to each other from afar. I detest technology that would render our lives easier and in reality, complicates it for us, or at least it squelches it, making it predictable and vulgar. I do not like to find myself in front of a screen. A glass screen, so arrogant it believes itself omnipotent, framed by aluminum that reflects light and keeps a swarm of wires that are entwined within well hidden.
  But, mom, emails arrive in the time you take a breath! How can you compare that with the slowness of snail mail? was my daughter Lori's comment.

That is exactly the beauty of it, Lori. Slowness has its own hidden but profound value: the slowness of thought, the slowness of the word, the slowness of writing, the great privilege in a time of careless swiftness; the slowness that plants its seeds in the flesh, stretches out its roots, grows, turns into a leaf, flower, tree, the breath of the universe. That is how I answered her, and I know that you are of the same mind.

Mom, you fly too high, careful not to break your neck when you fall, and besides you seem a lot older than your own mother who at sixty uses a computer, sends off emails at full blast, and you have no idea what she can do with a smartphone and chats! My daughter always wants to have the last word.

If she's having fun, let her be, I retorted, I'm all for freedom.

What freedom, that's backwardness, she replied, you live in a literary dimension and have no idea what the world is like, maybe you never did, mom.

As if the work I do and the responsibility I take on to keep the family afloat did not signal being aware of the world I pointed out to her.

At this point, the reckless little girl fell silent because she knows that without me, she would not have a roof over her head, food on the table, or even what is needed to buy a moped and pay for her schoolbooks. I say it not as a rebuke; it is just that I would like her to be a little more aware. But she is young; she is only seventeen. She will grow up soon enough.

I am working on the translation of *Madame Bovary*. And I am more and more convinced that the most humane person in the story is actually poor bullied

Charles, whom Flaubert treats as the last of the last. Yet he is the only one who knows how to love, the only one who suffers from Emma's death, the only one who does not deceive her and does not scorn and despise her. If he were not so awkward and clumsy, and if the author had not filled him with ridicule on every page, he would turn out to be a rather lovable character. When we see each other at Christmas, I want to read you the pages I have translated so far. It is a shame that in Italian, the sounds of the words are lost, words that for a perfectionist like Flaubert have a precise meaning, almost carnal I would say.

I again looked over the pictures of our last trip to Egypt, a little before the outbreak of the Arab Spring. One could almost smell something new in the air; you smelled that freedom, you understood immediately that something was happening. Too bad it ended so badly. Do you remember that evening on the floating restaurant with your friends, after dinner, when we looked out onto the Nile and your eyes were sparkling with joy? I like it when you are happy. I too suddenly feel happy. The river flowed by black and serene, the lights swung in its dark waters, the city reflected beautifully on that coffee-colored liquid and you recited a Baudelaire poem; I still remember the first verses which immediately stuck in my mind: *Sous une lumière blafarde / Court, danse et se tord sans raison / La Vie, impudente et criarde.* We heard far-off voices and you said that in that moment something grandiose was being decided: so many young people in search of freedom and no one would have stopped them, remember? Instead, they did stop them, damn it, and my, how they did stop them! Do you think the feeling of freedom is induced by culture or is it innate in each of us? I asked, and you answered, even a caged bird knows what freedom is, even if it cannot explain it.

Last night, I dreamed that you were phoning to tell me that you could not manage to fall asleep because a bird was pecking at your liver. Like Prometheus? I asked like a fool who reads too much. And you, who like me always has his nose stuck in a book, retorted that in Greek Prometheus means *he who reflects first*. But if he had first carefully thought about it, would Prometheus in fact have stolen fire from the gods of the skies? I wonder how many of us actually think before we act. You, for example, do not seem to me to be one who reflects first. While you are in the act of doing, perhaps you are reflective, but action requires a certain amount of recklessness, don't you think? Action requires momentum, determination: and if one reflects prior to taking action, what happens? One doubts, pushes back, maybe even gives up, which would not even be that bad if the action were harmful, but if the action is one of generosity, is it weakened by reflecting first? I would in fact say that you are one of those who reflect *while* they are doing things, not before—that is, you use thought as an instrument of knowledge, not as a mechanism of doubt. And at this point, I hear your voice saying: How do you know? Maybe I am more reflective than you think. I like your voice, François; you have a unique voice that I would recognize among thousands, a deep voice, seemingly opaque, almost anonymous, but then, in listening to it carefully, one can hear echoes within it that break up, expand as distant roots, and blossom as in a musical spell. You could have been an actor. You would have been very successful; I truly think so. Yours is a sensual voice, quiet, suitable for calm reasoning. You could

have been a philosopher or even a psychiatrist. With
that voice, you would be capable of calming a madman.
Instead, there you are, you have thrown yourself into
finance, you have set yourself to dealing with numbers.
I know your colleagues consider you a crazy intellectual
who eats up books and secretly writes meaningless poems,
but the fact is that you are a prisoner of that foolish
business, with limited vacation time.

Not too long ago, while reading one of your letters,
I heard your voice clear and festive, François, your voice
that makes me quake every time, especially when you
recite from memory the poems that you love so much:
Rimbaud, Baudelaire, Verlaine. You wallow in poetry,
as my daughter, Lori, would say; you drench yourself
in it, you come out soaked and happy. You remind me
of what a survivor of the Nazi extermination camps
recounted in a short book of memoirs that I translated
a few years ago.

Toward evening, after a horrible day of hard labor in
the camp, starving and hopeless, a few French friends would
gather together in the only place where the Nazis would not
go: the camp latrines, a disgusting, stinking place, with
a cement floor filthy with blood and urine, a stench that
took your breath away. The pretty SS lieutenants with
their pristine uniforms and shining boots were not at all
fond of that place of suffering and filth. Well, that's
exactly where our friends would gather to listen to poems
they had memorized when they were young boys. The
reciting voice was like a chant but a soft chant that could
not be heard outside the door, a rhythmic hum, and the
poems would miraculously give them the strength to go
on, you see, the strength to survive in that place of torture
and death.

I was very moved by this description and I believe to have learned from that story the kind of power that words can have when they become music and thought, a poignant and moving strategy of survival.

With much love, your
Maria

November 26

This morning I went to Mario's, he was sitting upright on his stool, in his lab coat, as he inserts needles into my back, he has chicken eyes, cold fixed and golden, his nose is running, his hand with the electric needle goes up and down following the design . . . he showed me through a mirror how the great feathered serpent of my future was coming along: it's swollen, red and black, and it blows out fire from its nostrils, just how I like it. Mario bites his lips with his teeth and works, he lets off an odor of sweat and coffee, I wouldn't have sex with him if he were the last man on earth, there's something about him that's like an underground rat, even if he is very talented in drawing on people's skin. Why do you want a dragon? he asked me with his chicken voice. Just because. Am I hurting you? I don't want to give him any satisfaction, the dragon is entering my skin, I feel it breathing and that's enough . . . who gives a shit about the pain?

11:00 A.M.

With the dragon still fresh on my back I swooped off to Tulù's place, I almost took a thirty-foot leap because I was distracted by a really good-looking guy who passed right in front of me and I hit a pothole on my moped. A chasm you mean, Tulù burst out laughing when I told him about it, that asshole, I had to ring the bell three times before he came to open the door, he turned the door handle, opened it a sliver looking all around as if he were expecting the police, his eyes peeking out from the crack, breathless. It's me, open up! Ah, it's you, Lori, come on in, what's up? you're all red in the face . . . I slip off my sweater and he's shocked. Who did it? Mario the Magician, I say, you remember he used to come to the coffeeshop at the tennis courts with us, he gave me a discount, like it? Hell yes, it looks real, this dragon is pissed, who does it want to scare? Whoever wants to attack me from behind, what do you think? What's it like? It's beautiful! How about we make love to celebrate? First I need some coffee. You want some? I've already had three cups, but let's go for a fourth, I like to watch Tulù as he messes around in the kitchen, which isn't actually a kitchen but a galley that doesn't even have any room for a table to put things on, and that's why he always keeps the balcony window door open where he placed a turned-over crate that he uses as a side table, the coffee tastes like shit, I tell him so, he laughs, luckily he's an easygoing guy, he's clumsy, but he has a nice hairless ass, *nonna* Gesuina judges people's character by their asses, she always tells me, since she gives people shots for a living she sees a whole lot of butts, she says that as soon as she uncovers one, she understands everything: if it's pointed, if it's hairy, if it's spotted with red blotches, if it easily gets goose bumps, if it's wrinkled like a turkey's neck, if it's nice and smooth and plump, she says that butts speak and she understands that language to perfection, Tulù's ass is beautiful, soft yet firm that you would eat it bite by bite, but he doesn't really like anyone to see him naked, he makes love by taking his underwear off at the last possible moment after having removed his shirt with slow and precise gestures, he hangs it on the back of the chair, he takes off his pants and folds them nice and neat and then he drapes them, without a wrinkle, on the chair, he likes slow things, done without haste: his shoes, one next to the other, never dusty or spotted, they look brand new like they just came from the store in that very moment, even his pajamas are nice and ironed, with all the buttons fastened, like this morning when he obviously was still sleeping when I got there, It's eleven o'clock and you're still in bed? I was up late, Lori, I don't feel like going to school today, Me neither, What did you say to your mother? Nothing, what do you want me to say, she doesn't listen to me anyway . . . she saw me take my jacket and backpack and leave, that's it, it wouldn't even occur to her that I skipped school, that I had an appointment with Mario the Magician to have a dragon tattooed on my back, my mother's an airhead, who knows what she's thinking about, if I had a job and didn't have to depend on her, I wouldn't stay a minute longer in that boring house with my mom and *nonna* all over me. Wasn't your grandmother an actress? She gave that up long ago, now she gives shots for a living, No more theater? Who wants a sixty-year-old woman? Well, sixty's not so old, my mother's sixty too, but dresses like a teenager and a lot of men chase after her, Your mother is your mother, and my grandmother is my grandmother, even if she still cares for it, don't believe it, she gave up acting, actually rather than giving it up, they fired her because she didn't go to rehearsals, she'd fall in love with all the actors who performed with her, and even with set people and she spent her time flirting behind the scenes, but, if you see her when she gets all dolled up, she looks twenty years younger, she's still very pretty, if she weren't nosy like a monkey and sly as a fox, she and I would get along really well, she knows how to tell a good story and, besides that, she's funny.

5:00 P.M.

Had my coffee, had sex with Tulù, it was so-so, I guess he doesn't really feel like it, I heard at school that he likes boys, maybe, seems to me he's just someone who's afraid of letting himself go and that's why he's awkward, he doesn't seem gay to me, he's a strange guy, he's shy at sex, eyes closed, in a hurry and without saying a word, I like his scent of ricotta and chamomile, he's like a newborn baby who's still suckling his mother's milk, I like that scent and so I close my eyes too and it's like rocking him: *hush-a-bye baby / on the tree top / when the wind blows / the cradle will rock* . . . a lullaby my *nonna* would sing to me in English when I was little, her English is pretty good, sometimes we chat and she teaches me a word here and there, she even speaks French, she's a powerhouse, my *nonna* is, I have no idea how she managed to bring an airhead like my mother into this world.

8:00 P.M.

Tulù and I laughed and laughed as we ate moldy cookies out on the balcony that overlooks other balconies full of plants, luckily no one ever sees us, and I say, You're always so tidy, couldn't you at least buy fresh cookies? These've expired! He just laughs, all that laughter could get on your nerves, if it weren't for his nice little cat teeth, clean and shiny, so sparkling that sometimes it makes me think of a shark, poor Tulù, so rich in family, but poor in thought, it's not that he's stupid, he's just withdrawn, wrapped up like a porcupine and if you get too close, he shows his quills, just as he was about to cum, he pulled out because he doesn't want to get me pregnant, he got a paper towel from the kitchen, wiped his semen from me, folded the towel into fours and again into fours, and he slipped it under the ashtray on the nightstand, but he doesn't even smoke so what use is that ashtray, who knows, maybe it's an ornament, the words *Welcome to Capri* with a blue sea painted on it, white foamy waves and a tiny boat.

10:00 P.M.

That's it, I'd like to have a tattoo of a boat that sails on high waves, I like the sea, I like to ride the waves of a rough sea, but then I saw that dragon on a balloon that was dancing in the wind and I thought, no, I want that, what are dragons anyway? Creatures that we invent ourselves, Tulù answered, do dragons exist? No. So where do they come from? From inside my head, inside yours, Tulù, except you would never have a dragon in your head, I think that in that darn head of yours you have neat bookcases with clocks, books that no one ever reads but are bound and other ashtrays that remind you of trips never taken.

11:00 P.M.

I don't like having sex in the morning anyway, there's always that smell of stale saliva and hair that stinks of a sweaty pillow, but two people who have known each other for years, who are schoolmates, who tell each other their business, what can they do first thing in the morning on a boring and unsurprising day? they have sex, it's not written anywhere, but they do it and that's it, maybe because there's nothing else to do, afterward you have a cup of coffee and then shower and in the end Tulù sits wrapped in a towel and eats his yogurt, but it has to be nonfat, he says, because he wants to watch his weight, and he buys everything at the organic store, my *nonna* calls it a jewelry store, because there a carrot that's more curved than straight will set you back three euros, can you believe it? does that even seem possible?

December 2

4:00 P.M.

Testing, testing, testing . . . one, two, one, two, three . . . have you started up, idiot tape recorder? One, two, one, two, testing, testing, testing! You couldn't be any smaller. I chose you because you were handy, easy to keep in my pocket, so that when I feel like it I turn you on, but don't be a pain. What's going on? Has the battery died? No, there, now it's on, but you're so slow, my little recorder! So are we ready? What a fucking day! I slept poorly, got up late. When I went to the baker for a warm croissant, there were a bunch of people and I had to wait. Simone was at the counter, all sweaty from the swift moves he had to make to pull the bread off the shelves, wrap it up, take the money, give back change, pull another loaf out, open another bag, throw in the bread, take the money, and so on. When he saw me, he smiled, but a crooked and exhausted smile. Seems like everyone is in a hurry today, elbowing one another to get their bread and leave. I would have stayed the whole day long in the midst of that lovely scent of fresh-baked bread, watching Simone's rapid movements, his bare muscular arms, his long sweaty neck, his curly hair that fell onto his forehead, his lovely hands that run from one baguette to the next, his mouth with its round lips, his big, gentle eyes. What are you always at that baker's for? asks my granddaughter Lori who is nosy and prying. I like the baker, what's wrong with that? My grand-daughter spies on me, but I let her, she's as gossipy as a mos-quito, she buzzes and buzzes and then she stings you. But I let her buzz. A little vampire to tell the truth, but she loves me, I know, we get along, the two of us, unlike that airhead of a daughter of mine. Maria is as fragile as a freshly laid egg. Barely touch her and she'll break. Yet she has the perfection of an egg that is smooth, sealed, and flawless. It's just that if you place it on the table, it rolls away and then it cracks.

My granddaughter understands me, she backs me up, she's my accomplice. The other day I had the baker come to the house with the excuse that he needed to help me bring about five pounds of bread home. I had him come in and then, behind the kitchen door, we quickly kissed, without even an embrace. Lori was on the lookout on the other side of the door. Normally she keeps her mouth shut and smiles. This time though she attacked me: Do you realize he's just a boy, he's my age and you could be his grandmother! If he's attracted to me as I am to him, what can I do about it? I answered but with the tone of someone who is trying to justify herself, when in fact I should be defending more forcibly the freedom of love that knows no age, that makes bread, sweat, gasp, breath, heat, excitement, all because of the pleasure of the game of love. I should be more decisive, more convincing, and instead I always pay homage to my granddaughter Lori's youthful arrogance.

Maria's back with her grocery bags. I used the excuse of heavy bags. The baker was embarrassed and so was I, but Maria never notices anything, even if she were to find me in my underwear with the baker naked, she would make a beeline for her writing table to stick her nose in her books, as if she were blindfolded. Maria is as distracted as a winter rose, a walking disaster, but it's also true that she financially supports us with her translations, paid in paltry sums, to tell the truth, but paid on time. She finally found a serious publisher after so many skinflints, people who made her work like a slave and then had her wait six months before giving her what she was owed. And in the meantime? Debts with the grocer, debts with the fruit vendor, debts

with the fishmonger, after a while they look disapprov-
ingly. And besides, I believe it won't be long before we
won't be able to buy anything more on credit because all
the shops are beginning to disappear, along with all the
Andrews, Matthews, Georges who would otherwise give me
credit. Now only supermarkets are opening and there goes
my credit, you have to pay on the spot. Luckily my reputation as a nurse has spread. An actress turned nurse? It's
laughable, as my granddaughter says. In all the years on
stage, in addition to acting I also learned how to heal the
sick, to give shots, so what's wrong with that? I have the
soul of a doctor, I like to poke around sick bodies, I like to
understand where the illness lies, I like to find, actually I
would say *invent* cures. I should have gone to medical
school instead of that stupid academy, but my mother was
against it, and everyone kept telling me I was a born actress,
and yet no—I was a born doctor except I wasn't allowed to
study medicine. I'm the injection wizard, this I can state
with pride. And I judge people by their asses, as I explained
to my granddaughter. Depending on the type of butt they
have, I can even tell whether they'll pay right away or not.
On the ones who will not pay right away I'm tempted to
leave a nice bruise, but I don't, for the love of the profession, I have to keep my reputation as queen of the syringe.
I place the needle on the butt, which I divide into four sec-
tions with an imaginary pen, and I aim for the top quad-
rant, tap with two fingers and the needle penetrates with
pleasant ease. Then I pull up on the plunger to make sure I
haven't hit a capillary. Then I slowly inject the liquid. When
I've placed the alcohol-soaked cotton on the punctured skin,
they say to me: What? Already done? Yes, all done, you
didn't feel a thing, did you? No, absolutely nothing. And I
gloat because that butt will talk to other butts and then all

the butts of the neighborhood will get in line to have me prick them.

My granddaughter had a dragon tattooed on her back. *Nonna*, look, she said to me lifting up her sweater. A beautiful dragon: an enormous, huge snake with golden scales, proud head, a purple crest, mouth opened wide with flames spilling out. I would never know how to make such a thing even with my skill with needles. Well, of course, it's one thing to work with tattoos and quite another to give injections. Still, they do have one thing in common: the needle. It's a matter of injecting a liquid into the body. The only difference is that in one case the liquid serves to define and color the illness, while in the other the liquid serves to color and define a dream on the flesh. One acts on the innards, the other on the skin. They're relatives, in short, distant cousins, let's put it that way.

I met a young man on the internet. He says he's thirty years old, but who knows? they all tell lies in there. Besides, I even lied, I said I was forty. Twenty years younger. I quickly learned that you have to do that. Maybe the fun is precisely in hiding yourself behind different masks. Even if Pirandello says that when one mask falls, another is always revealed. I've about a hundred different masks and I have fun changing them up. Besides, I'm crazy about playing around: people don't know how to play anymore, but I like taking risks, placing my bet on red or black and then waiting for the surprise of winning or losing. I don't care about losing, I enjoy what comes before. The anticipation, in short, is the most exciting thing in the world: that balancing act over the precipice: will I fall in headfirst or will I land with my feet on the ground, indeed, to find a pocketful of gold coins? I'm not talking about gambling; I'm talking about the game of love. I always take a risk and often lose, but sometimes I win.

Even in the theater, you win and you lose, but more often than not you end up in the fog of the indistinct. I like the disease that comes with the theater: the disease of solitude, of wandering, of living with strangers, of constant pretending. All diseases of the spirit that at times make you deliriously happy, at times depressed and wishing only to die. Lori says that they fired me because I didn't follow the rules, because I flirted—she doesn't understand the game of love—with my colleagues just to pass the time, just so I wouldn't get too bored. It's just that they applaud an eighty-year-old stage actor even if he can barely stand, a woman on the other hand, they kick out on her ass. How could the audience possibly be interested in a lopsided and withered body? The fact is I have nothing you could call withered, I'm a walking sixty-year-old miracle, want to see my legs? The fact is in the theater they consider a sixty-year-old woman already a centenarian. Only when a scene requires a centenarian, maybe the part is yours. But what can a centenarian do? Just a cameo. Can a centenarian have the leading role in a play? In the entire history of the theater there has not been a leading-lady centenarian. And so, get out, shoo, don't bust my balls!

And that's how I ended up getting paid to give shots. It would lead me to suicide if it weren't for my sense of humor. I concentrate on the geography of moles at the bottom of a back, and I see them as constellations: Cassiopeia, the Big Dipper and the Little one, the North Star, there are people who have a bunch of moles on their glutes, and then there are the pimples that I see as small volcanoes ready to erupt and those folds in the fatty flesh that look like traces of ancient waterways. I have fun making those asses talk.

I then tell my granddaughter about it and she listens attentively. My daughter is too prudish to follow the language of butts. She frowns even if I merely utter the word *ass*, let alone the rest of it. Someone like her who reads so much and always has her nose stuck in a book is scandalized if you use a lewd word, but what's lewd about an ass? what would you want to call an ass? ass, right? it's as if I'd want to change the names of pots and pans because they are so commonplace. So, if I wanted a frying pan, I shouldn't say, "I'm looking for a frying pan," but rather, "I'm looking for something made of iron in the form of a disc." Ridiculous, right? No one would understand me. Or a hammer, what should I call that? a piece of wood with a parallelepiped attached on top? Bullshit!

You could use the word *buttocks*, my daughter, Maria the prude, says, but it's too overdressed a word, it lacks the nudity that reveals itself as it awaits the peck of a light and expert hand as mine. Let's just say that an ass is an ass and there's nothing wrong with pronouncing that word, even children hear it willingly: Doesn't every mom say: clean your little ass, my love? So where's the scandal in that? But my daughter is a boring boiled potato, a potato in love with that dapper little Frenchman, that financial officer with big hands and small feet, with whom she sets off on vacation to explore the world. Last year they went to Egypt, just barely escaping being beaten up by a crowd of crazed young men. The year before to India: Calcutta, Varanasi. Maria brought back a bunch of pictures; so very banal to tell the truth, but taken with a real camera, no cell phone, no selfies, the two plantigrades do not like technological sophistication at all. But they do go on airplanes. And I bet they made their hotel reservations through the internet. But maybe not, those two are capable of arriving in Varanasi without having reserved a thing, ending up in a squalid B and B that stinks of shit and a mile away, where they steal everything as soon as you turn your back.

December 15

Dear François,

My mother left the house speaking, whispering actually into her portable tape recorder. Even Lori has gone out, slamming the door as usual. What could she want to tell me with that bang that makes me jump each time? That she can no longer stand this place, her grandmother, the poverty we live in, the privations we suffer, me who translates all day long, that I am not a good breadwinner and perhaps not even a good mother? She could just tell me herself, and sometimes she does, but that door slamming is a more decisive language and goes straight to the brain passing like a poisoned arrow through my ears.

It makes me think of the door slammed by Mme Chauchat—do you remember *The Magic Mountain*?—the woman who would always come late to the dining hall in the sanatorium and slam the door so that everyone would snap their heads up to look at her, who, elegantly dressed, haughty and beautiful, would slide between the tables? And Hans Castorp, the man in love with her, who kept her chest X-rays in his pocket, to tease a kiss from her, do you remember? Recollections of literary passages for a voracious reader like me intertwine with lived moments, funny, is it not? They get mixed up and intertwined as if I had experienced them myself: that door that she slams rings in my ears and belongs to me just as other personal memories belong to me. Is it an advantage or a curse? I am asking it of another voracious reader, therefore the answer is not valid, it lacks objectivity. But does objectivity exist, my love? I would say of course not. As we say here, everyone pulls water to his own mill. So long as the mill grinds and produces flour, otherwise what is it but a pure game of water?

I am all alone in an empty house. I like when I am alone in the quiet of this isolated room where I sleep at night. I would very much have liked a study with all my books on the walls, but the house is not big enough. The three of us have a room each, nothing more. There is only one bathroom, one kitchen. If I want to write, I have to make do with a small table shoved in between my bed and the window, next to the small sofa that I pushed up against the wall. Luckily, the bathroom is next to my door and I can go in and out as I please, except when Lori locks herself in there to smoke her stinking cigarettes.

I love being alone with you on this sheet of paper that will travel ever so slowly and arrive at your house in Lille. I kiss your hoarse, delicious voice. I have to leave you to return to the translation that awaits me.

Till soon, I hope.

A most tender embrace, your
Maria

December 16

I come back and find my mother writing a letter, she doesn't use a computer of course, my adorable little mama, there she is in her baggy pants, in her big, torn sweater, seated in her orthopedic, padded swivel chair, writing a letter with a pen, ladies and gentlemen! not with a ballpoint pen but with a real-life fountain pen, otherworldly stuff, and she has to refill it all the time with that black liquid, and if you swipe it with your finger it smudges the whole sheet of paper, but she likes it like that, my mom's old-fashioned. And who's she writing to anyway? I'm just saying because I already know she's writing to that ridiculous Frenchman who phones every once in a while and calls her "mon amour," they've been writing to each other for years and every three or four months they see each other when the ridiculous one has some vacation time, leaves Lille where he works and comes to Italy, they rent a car together and go around like tourists: they hold hands while visiting the temples in Agrigento, or the Roman villas in Pompei, or the *calli* in Venice, I saw the pictures, she keeps them hidden, My things, she says embarrassed, who are you kidding, mom, you're crazy in love, you and the Frenchman make me laugh with all your schmaltzy lovey-dovey-ness, *nonna* and I looked at all the photos one day when you weren't home and we laughed our heads off: two forty-year-olds who dive into the sea over the Gargano and synchronize swim and then kiss on a rock that seems to have sprung up from the water just for them . . . can anyone be more absurd! at home, on the other hand, books and more books and then even more books, we're full of paper, classics and modern, there's something for everyone's liking, because my very intelligent mother reads like a bookworm, she's always got her nose stuck in the pages of a book, we have hundreds of them, and it seems like even he, François de Lille, reads a lot, in fact when they take off they fill their luggage with books, two crazies, and in exchange they may be missing a clean pair of socks.

The dragon's telling me it's fed up with being shut up at home, it wants to go out but I have homework to do! You'll do it later, c'mon let's go! So we go out, but where to? It pressed against my shoulder blades and I fly down the stairs, hop onto my moped and race off like crazy, I like the wind in my face and the dragon likes it too, plastered onto my back, when it's happy it blows out colored flames, I can see curls of smoke that come out from under my arms, I know it's the dragon who's happily getting excited, it twists like a worm and eats up pounds of air, he really likes sucking in air and then throwing it out in the form of a cloud or of smoke, I race and race but I don't know where I'm headed, it knows, the dragon, pushing me on behind my shoulders but when we turn toward the outskirts, I finally realize we're going to the former public park, now transformed into a garbage dump, we're heading there to say hi to the old tramp who lives under the bushes, I reach for my pocket to see if I have my wallet with me, luckily it's there, safe and sound, the dragon presses on, I race through a red light risking an accident, but who cares, I stop at the corner café and order a double cappuccino, nice and hot inside a Styrofoam cup with a vacuum-sealed cover and I slip two croissants into a bag, I get to the park as the sun is beginning to go down and flies are everywhere, the tramp greets me opening her toothless mouth, I get down from my moped, and sit next to her as she's preparing some powdered milk in some cold water inside a jar she found who knows where.

I brought you a hot cappuccino, actually two, and she, as a way of thanking me, plants a kiss on my cheek with her sticky mouth. No kisses, do you need money? she doesn't answer but looks at me with suspicion: what does this crazy little girl want, offering me money as if I were a tramp? she feels like the queen of the ex–public park, now abandoned and serving as a waste deposit, she lives there as if it were a house, in the midst of broken bikes, mattresses chewed up by rats, smashed refrigerators, she lives there as the absolute owner and she doesn't understand what I want from her, experience tells her that if someone approaches her, they want to insult her or scold her or even hit her and send her away or maybe just preach to her, she's used to being scorned or mistreated, she doesn't expect anything good from anyone who draws near, they're there either to steal what little she has, or to hit her over the head telling her to get out of there because she stinks and she makes the city ugly, I timidly offer her the Styrofoam cup which she looks at suspiciously, but then she suddenly grabs it from my hand and gulps it down, don't you want the croissants? she grabs those from my hand too but then she hides them, she'll eat them later when she's hungry, she has solid locks of white hair that look like they're sculpted from marble and two big, beautiful eyes of an angel who has just closed the doors of a too tidy and boring Paradise, she stays here in this garbage pit for her convenience, waiting, for what I have no idea, she eats without chewing, swallowing down whole bites exactly like the seagull that comes to visit me on my house balcony, it knows I bring it bread, grapes, cookies, it looks at me with those evil eyes and stretches out its neck to grab the piece of cookie I have in my hand, but it doesn't hurt me, it's delicate with that homicidal beak that could poke out one of my eyes, it grabs what I bring it and eats it in one gulp without chewing at all. But don't you have any teeth? I ask it and it stretches out its neck to take a piece of pizza I have in my hand: it's gentle and discreet, that seagull that when it spreads its wings must be six feet wide, it looks exactly like this toothless tramp who gulps down croissants and then works with her throat as if she were mincing them up with her esophagus, I don't know why I come to visit this filthy tramp with dirty hands, greasy and oily hair that sticks up from the filth, she creeps me out, still I come because the dragon wants me to, yeah, now I can say that it's the one that forced me to come here,

Do you hear me, Goldie? the old woman has a name, she confessed it to me one frigid morning when I brought her a blanket, her name's Goldie, It sounds like the name of a fish, I say and she laughs, that toothless mouth gives me goose bumps and yet, I take her hand and squeeze it because I want to make her understand that I find her likable, even if she disgusts me, What do you think you are, a fledgling Franciscan? I can hear my *nonna*'s voice teasing me, I turn around but there's no one there, it's the dragon who's imitating Gesuina's voice like a parrot and I'm the one who's laughing this time and I take out my wallet and hand over a twenty to Goldie, she opens her eyes wide like a fish out of water, and maybe this time she understands that I don't want anything from her, I don't want to beat her up, don't want to spit in her face, don't want to throw her out of her den in the garbage heap, with an easy gesture she throws the Styrofoam cup over her shoulder onto the pile of rubbish, grabs the twenty and then she turns away from me and goes back to tinkering with a piece of rusted bicycle, Bye! I say and she doesn't answer, hunched over an iron she's trying to transform into something useful, I say Bye! again, waiting for a response that doesn't come, I get back on my moped and head home.

December 17

Dear François,

I have just returned from the doctor who says I have chronic colitis on account of my nerves. I was hunched over in pain this morning. That is why I left halfway through the translation which I had been working on nonstop. I should walk more, concentrate less on books, eat more slowly and only food that is cooked, nothing raw which irritates the intestines, above all never canned foods opened at the last minute, no wine, no fresh fruit, and then rest, rest, rest, the doctor insists. But how can I rest if I have to submit a translation of nearly four hundred pages in a few days? What's more, I have to go grocery shopping because I cannot count on my mother, nor my daughter. It is up to me to cook, keep the house clean. At least they make their own beds. Even if Lori limits herself to simply pulling up the bedspread. My mother, on the other hand, smooths out the bedsheets and even changes them often, saying she wants things to have a just-washed smell, and who then does the laundry? But I bought you a washing machine! she says in a huff, throwing in my face the ten-year-old gift she got me in a moment of glory after a television cameo that paid well and up front. But the clothes don't go in the machine by themselves, you have to separate them into whites and colors, put in the detergent, make sure it starts off well, and then take them out all tangled, hang them out to dry and finally iron them once they are dry. Even if by now I iron almost nothing because I simply do not have the time. I fold the clothes and place them in the dresser. Sometimes my mother, as a way of reprimanding me, takes to ironing while belting out a song.

But I do not wish to bore you with the stories of a house full of women. Three generations of females who put up with one another out of necessity. And yet, if my mother and daughter were to disappear, I would feel desperately alone. Family ties are complicated and hatch unknown consequences. We love one another madly, but we also detest one another. We find the gestures, actions, choices made by those who live with us intolerable, but at the same time we dread the thought of when this intimacy will end. Lori will get married sooner or later, even if it is still too soon, but I see her restless and eager to leave. My mother will die, even though based on the vitality she displays, I believe she will live another fifty years or so. And there you have it, I'm fretful, you tell me so yourself: you worry too much, Maria, let yourself go, do not consume yourself over others, think of yourself, get more sleep, take care of yourself, let them unravel their own lives, if you were not around, what would they do?

You are right. But my ant-like nature, gathering morsels to bring back to the colony, forces me to rush around from morning till night, up and down what look to me like insurmountable mountains and instead may be small bumps in the road depending on one's point of view, right? I translated a book last year that talked about time. The thousands, millions of years that the galaxies have been around, the solar system that races precipitously with billions of stars that turn on and off, what do they mean for us? In the end we must realize that we live as long as a fruit fly that dies after a few hours. It is just that we have learned the art of measuring that inhuman and atrocious thing that we call time, we have learned to give it meaning, a perspective, and that is why life spreads out in front of us, it lengthens, it gloriously protracts. And besides, we invented that poetic and harrowing object that is the clock. We scrutinize and measure the hours, the minutes, the seconds on that white dial, and we seem to think ourselves masters of that time that guides us and regulates our lives. But time does not exist, François, we are at the mercy of chaos, and just like for that fruit fly for whom two minutes equals two hundred years, even human beings deceive themselves in a way that one day becomes one year, one year fifty, one hundred years. What luxury!

I love you, François, do not pay attention to the ruminations of an anxious woman, perplexed in the face of the times of the universe. We are here in the meantime, we are ephemeral but in love, and that is all that matters for us, does it not?

Yours,
Maria

December 18

Christmas preparations have begun, what a pain! my mom's got a fire up her butt because she has to turn in her four hundred pages of that totally lame book by Flaubert and it's late, she almost never sleeps at this point: she's up till one or two in the morning glued to that desk and in the morning she's already awake at six o'clock with a dictionary in her hand, while *nonna*'s still snoring and I've just gotten up to pee, but then I crawl back to bed for a while, even with my eyes closed I see her face that looks like a desperate turtle who's writing and writing mercilessly.

What would you like for Christmas, Tulù asks me, he's such a perfectionist and wants to know everything ahead of time, Well, I'd like . . . but I stop there because I truly don't know what I need, Tell me something you like, there must be something you're interested in, Yes, a dog, I'd really like a dog to hold in my arms, to take for walks, a dog I can run with, jump with, I don't know, I've always wanted one, but my mom doesn't agree because she says you then have to take care of it, And who's going to feed it, give it water, take it out? I'll do it all, mom, don't worry about it! You bet I'm worried because I know very well how it'll end up: you'd keep it in your room, shedding everywhere and then you'd go out on your moped leaving the dog behind and it would fall on me to take the dog out, clean the sidewalk and feed it, I know you all too well, But there are three of us, including *nonna*, couldn't she take the dog out? Your grandmother can't be trusted, is that clear? and that's the end of the discussion, there's no way to make her change her mind, But, Lori, tell me what you would like for Christmas, she even asks me . . . why don't you all just give presents without all these questions! and I already know that she'll end up giving me two or three books, which honestly she'll just end up reading herself because I leave them lying around, after a while books bore me, at some point while I'm reading the letters start to dance like flies swirling around, so I stop, leave the book on the couch face down and open on the page I was reading, that's where my mom finds it and she grumbles at me, but I answer her in kind You want me to be a carbon copy of you, mom, and you're wrong because I'm not at all like you, I'm not self-righteous, all books and cooking who writes love letters to a shitty Frenchman who only knows how to send kisses: has he ever even given you a present, I mean a single worthwhile present? I don't want presents, she says, as proud as a peacock, the love of a man like François is a gift unto itself, mom you've fallen into the oldest and darkest love trap just like any ordinary schoolgirl, You're wrong, Lori, for six years now I am loved in return by the same man and we do many things besides write to each other, we plan trips, we travel the world, we are free and happy, Lucky you, I answered, but in the meantime I'd like to beat her head against the wall because she's worse than a little girl: love doesn't exist, do you understand, mom, neither does the world that's about to go to pieces like an old balloon full of air and wind.

December 19

Dear François,

This is a curious house: I write letters, my daughter writes a diary she keeps hidden in a hole in the wall, my mother records what she has on her mind into a tiny tape recorder that she hides in her pocket. Sometimes I hear her talking and talking as though she were interrogating herself. I even hear her laughing, fortunately she's a cheerful woman, this is not a house of curmudgeons, but of argumentative women, yes, because we are always bickering with one another, something inevitable, I suppose, in a family of such different personalities.

My daughter, in a gesture of great generosity, offered her computer to me so I could speak with you via "Skaip," she says it is the fastest and cheapest way for me to see your face and hear you. But I told her no, a most emphatic no. How can I make her understand that distance is a poetic circumstance? The absence that we nurture through the written word—do we want to crush that with that vulgar thing that is a kind of telephone with moving pictures? My imagination is much more powerful than that gadget made of iron and glass. I see you while I write and I see your hands as they move on the page, and I smell the scent of your body, and I listen to your voice that answers me, questions me, caresses me. It is so, so much more rewarding to dream through the written word than through a diabolic machine that seems to draw people near while distancing them at the same time.

You told me that you would be coming for Christmas. Is there something that is stopping you now? I am already planning our New Year's Eve dinner. I would like for you to be with us at least once. Now that your mother has died, can I hope that you will join us? What would you like to eat? Do you like crayfish? Or do you prefer stuffed turkey? My mother is quite good at chestnut stuffing with bacon and raisins. Shall I tell her to prepare it? Lori announced that she wants to make dessert, but I do not trust her. With that dragon on her shoulders she seems to have become more brazen and ready to fly away.

Flaubert drives me crazy. Why did he say *I am Emma Bovary*, if he then goes and abuses her, despises her and considers her an enemy? Was he an enemy to himself? At times I think so. He uses pages and pages to pick on Emma's exoticism and then he reveals himself to be more attached to exotic dreams than his own character is. Was he castigating Emma for something that he hated in himself? And why does he make every effort to portray as hateful and treacherous the poor woman who then, paradoxically, everyone considers a heroine of feminine freedom? The scene with her old wet nurse to whom she entrusted her own nursing daughter is disgusting. Emma goes to visit her daughter in the ugly and very shabby country house where she has exiled her, takes her in her arms, says a few sweet words to her, but as soon as the newborn spits up on her, she becomes enraged, puts her down in the shabby, dirty crib, and thinks only of cleaning her shirt collar, no longer caring at all about the baby. And when her daughter, now six years old, hugs her legs with too much vigor, Emma shoves her away such that the child falls to the floor hitting her head against the edge of a table and begins to bleed. This young mother, this Emma with beautiful white arms and an angelic smile, what does she do? Instead of bending over and picking her daughter up from the floor, and apologizing for that shove, she gracelessly sticks a bandage on her while scolding her, and when her husband arrives, she accuses her daughter of having fallen on her own, because the little girl is clumsy and inept, hiding the fact that it was she who made her fall. And the time when she looks at her wounded daughter as she is sleeping and comments: How ugly this child is! In short, Emma demonstrates that she is not only a terrible mother, but even an insensitive, egotistical person, devoid of gentleness. Is this what Gustave wanted? A man himself unhappy, true, in his provincial life that he detested, but to which he remained faithful for love of his mother, by whom he was dominated and in love, so much as to hide from her his relationship with Louise, and forced the poor woman to write to him at a friend's address. And when Louise, despite all the prohibitions, decides to go and visit him, he leaves her outside the door and insults her in front of his mother. Behavior of a weak man or a vile one? And when his mother forbids him from going out on the boat, because of her long-standing fear of his epilepsy, Gustave, who loves rowing so much, does not say a word, he obeys, putting away his beloved boat and oars for good. And yet, his books do not depict repressive and tyrannical mothers. Must Emma pay for that tyranni-cal mother who tormented him in her belief that she was protecting her son?

I would very much like to have a good conversation with you, listening to your wise voice, a great reader and connoisseur of French literature. But tell me without delay whether you can manage to come for Christmas. I am expecting you. In that way you will get to know Lori better, whom you have only met at the door one or two times. She is always in a rush with her moped, as are you with your trains and planes. For once, instead of celebrating Christmas with your mother, we could dine as a family and then take off for someplace all our own, even if I fear that the places where one can enjoy some peace and quiet are becoming ever scarcer because the world is ravaged by wars, by crises, by the flight of people from countries infested by terrorism, disease and hunger. What do you think about going to Holland? For once, a destination not too far away, a land you do not know, where I have been once before but for a short time with my husband before he died. We could go see the Van Gogh paintings you love so much. A place that lives on the water's edge, and that has a symbiotic relationship with the sea, would you like that?

But I must get back to my translation, even if I feel bad leaving you. I draw you in with open arms and then close them in a gesture of most tender love.

Yours,
Maria

December 19

Mom, c'mon, are you writing to that boring François again? When one loves, one loves forever, my child! Aren't you bored yet with this guy who's far away and writes you paper letters like an old fart? Well, I like paper, and so does François, he places his hands here, don't you understand? and I smell the scent of his skin on this piece of paper, Mom, your sentimentalism is disgusting! What do you care, it's my business, I know but I'm telling you you're a wreck, when I treat her like that, she shrivels up into her shoulders like a frightened bird . . . do I scare her? I don't think so, but maybe I frighten her to the point that she doesn't recognize me: When and where did I give birth to this child who is so different from me? I actually believe she's thinking that when she hides inside her shoulders and turns her back on me to once again take up writing those stupid love letters.

Talked to *nonna* for a long time about the tramp who lives in the middle of all that trash and even of Tulù, but she could care less about the tramp, she doesn't find her interesting, instead she's quite interested in Tulù, Will you introduce me to him? she says, And why should I? I don't know, just to meet him . . . but I immediately get the message: she wants to meet him so she can flirt with him, Fuck, *nonna*, aren't you ashamed, at your age? I don't force myself on them, I don't rape them, I limit myself to caressing them with my eyes, I tell them they're handsome, that they have wonderful skin, that they have eyes like headlights and they're so happy that they agree to a date, but nothing ever happens, I'm not that crazy to expect to have sex with boys who could very well be my grandsons, all I ask is to look them over, so I can admire them, and if it goes really well, I earn a kiss, A kiss, *nonna*? you behave worse than a bedeviled male, You're wrong, it has nothing to do with the devil, simply a very sweet woman in love with love, You act like a she-wolf, but you're not a wolf, you're an old lady and no one wants you, And yet, I attract them like honey, my child, in my opinion these poor boys feel lonely, no one listens to them, no one takes them seriously, no one tells them they are handsome, attractive, sensual, and they feel so totally surprised to hear themselves praised that they almost fall in love, And you take advantage of that to fuck them! I yell with my sword unsheathed, ready to strike, Of course not, you fool, consummate love is for the young and I'm not interested, I fill my eyes with those bodies and I'm content, a few kisses at the most, just so as not to leave them disappointed, A few kisses, *nonna*? you really are a degenerate, and you want to do that with my Tulù? No, of course not, I was just kidding, I won't touch your Tulù, you can have him all to yourself.

That is my grandmother, Gesuina, a woman who knows how to handle a man, me on the other hand, so much younger than her, I'm not at all good at it; it's because she never gets embarrassed, she moves about confidently, convinced, and she manages to convince others too, *Nonna*, you're a marvel! and she laughs, she musters up that actor's voice of hers and, just like that, she recites the role of Mirandolina, which she knows by heart, having played her when she was a girl during a long stage tour that took her all over Italy, she must have been good too, because they must have performed Goldoni's *Locandiera* at least three hundred times in three hundred different theaters, then she fell in love with an asshole of an actor who ended up getting her pregnant and that was the end of Mirandolina for her, he got sick and she cared for him for years, up until he died, poor *nonno*, I never even met him, *nonna* says he was a great actor and people applauded and clapped their hands raw, we're left with a few photos, but they're posed portraits, black and white: a tall man, neither handsome nor ugly, with a phenomenal mustache and a type of feathered military hat on his head, *Nonna*, tell me something about him, I like to hear her talk about my grandfather, the actor Giacomo Cascadei for whom people would applaud their hands raw, What do you want me to say? He was handsome, he had a wonderful voice, he knew how to move on stage, but he was a wimp like few others: when I told him I was pregnant, he immediately denied the child was his, Look, I want a kid over my dead body, besides it wasn't me, who knows who else you fucked, you're a woman without morals, without scruples, who knows what you did! I loved him so much, and I had only ever been with him, so

I put up with it and just kept repeating: Look, it's yours and yours alone, I was a virgin when I met you, and I didn't sleep with anyone but you, but he didn't believe it, he saw me as flighty, easy and he thought I would go to bed with anyone, instead I was a fool who didn't even take any precautions because I was a naive silly girl and knew nothing of love, go figure if I would even think of anyone except him! Now though you're making up for all that candor and ignorance about sex, *nonna*, Now yes, I'm an adult and am well aware, I know my desires, and I try my best to satisfy them, I don't expect much, but a little, yes, sex doesn't die at sixty, just ask sixty-year-old men, even eighty, they think it's their right to desire and bed a young girl, we women are not allowed to even look at a nice body without immediately turning into witches, whores, good-for-nothings, bedeviled, as you say, That's old school, *nonna*, today's sixty-year-old women get what they want! You'll understand when you turn sixty, she answered me brusquely.

There you have it, my grandfather was that man, tall, thin, with a handlebar mustache and close-knit eyes, a bit like a falcon's, an eagle's nose and two large peasant hands, in fact he was the son of peasants, They both stank of sheep, both his father, Aidan, as well as his wife, Rosalina, *nonna* Gesuina says, even though my ambitious parents wanted me to study so I went to the academy, at first I wanted to become a surgeon, but since it cost too much to send me to medical school, I chose the theater, they thought that I should have been a teacher, at most a pediatrician, but I stuck to my guns: I learned to speak well, leaving the dialect behind in the paternal countryside and I behaved like a city girl, and so did he, my schoolmate at the academy, the tall, handsome young man spoke a crisp Italian with no accent, but when I became pregnant, the scared sheepherder revealed himself and he denied, denied and didn't want to hear anything about the child, *Nonna*, but didn't *nonno* eventually recognize my mother as his? Yes, after she was born, after she had grown up and everyone said how much she looked like him, she was his spitting image and only on his deathbed, with all the relatives insisting, did he marry me and recognize your mother, Maria, as his own.

December 21

Will you turn on, stupid little machine? I have something lovely to tell you.

Yesterday, the doorbell rings. I go to open the door and there in front of me is a handsome man, his hair a little gray at the temples, but truly handsome, with a small pointed nose, big sad, oddly colored, violet-like eyes, fleshy pinkish smiling lips, two long arms like an orangutang's, an athletic body and no belly, can you believe it, no flabby belly, a rare thing nowadays: at a certain age they all develop a belly, they swell up like a balloon. Who knows why men develop such big bellies, so protruding it's like they have a longing for a child, as though they'd like to say: look, this is not all flab, inside here there's a beautiful baby girl who can't wait to be born so she can throw her arms around my neck, but in the meantime I'm keeping her sheltered from indecent glances, me and her, she and I, my wonderful little baby girl and I am her dad, how about that? Dads would like all women to remain forever little children, small, fragile, innocent, kind, loving, clingy, in need of protection: if you think of it, you'll see that in every American love song, the lover addresses the object of his love by calling her *my baby*, isn't that odd? They adore you as long as you're wearing little shoes with white ankle-high socks, as long as your breasts are barely noticeable under your blouse, as long as your hair falls down to your shoulders on its own without thinking of the color, the style, just as it normally falls, and your eyes, those eyes are adorable when they express innocence, trust, modesty. Oh, yes, that is a desirable girl, they would marry her in an instant. As soon as a woman starts to have body hair, as her bosom grows, as she begins to look directly in front of her, they no longer can stand them: who is that fat-ass, stuck-up girl? Where did you put that delightful, shy and quiet little girl who was inside you? Where did you chase off that bashful and enchanting child, innocent and afraid as you once were? I don't know who you are anymore, you shave your legs, you pluck your eyebrows, you read love stories and adventure novels, you start dreaming of things greater than yourself and then you claim to calculate, measure, evaluate, and even judge the other by yourself, in short, disgusting. Why didn't you stop yourself earlier? Why did you allow those pubic hairs to curl and the hair in your armpits to grow, why did you allow that roundness to form, that heaviness, don't you get that you take away any appetite I had?

That's what they think and the older they get the more they think like that, while boys, ah yes, boys are saved because they don't yet know the historical privileges of their sex. They like very much to be taken seriously, to be admired, praised, pampered, and even sometimes paid, and you know, they're always broke, I take this into account, but without laying claim to who knows what, just for the pleasure of smelling that flower and taking that bit of honey I manage to reach without excessive disturbances and annoyances to both sides.

Oh my, I'm tired of speaking. I'm a one-man band as my granddaughter, Lori, would say. And come to think of it, I don't understand why they gave her the name Loredana, to then just turn around and call her Lori. She looks more and more like her grandfather Giacomo Cascadei the cynic, the great, the desired, the egocentric Cascadei, always on tour, always admired, always applauded. My bedfellow, my fellow traveler, first by bus, then train and finally by car with a chauffeur no less, the great Cascadei could afford it, except that he spent and spent so much that when he died all he left was debt.

Wait, I was forgetting to say what happened this morning: I opened the door and there in front of me is this great-looking guy and I must have had a quizzical look on my face because he smiled (the smile of an angel who flies low and lands on a tree to peek through the windows) and he said to me: I'm François, don't you recognize me? Hell no, I had not recognized him: the last time I saw him he was at the door, wearing an ugly beret drawn down over his forehead, and he had a Band-Aid on his cheek for who knows what burned off mole so who could recognize him? Ah, is that you, François? I said to him, come in, come in, so nice to see you again. I wanted to add: my, you are handsome, damn you! But I resisted. He came in still smiling, putting down his suitcase. Where's Maria? She went to the market but she'll be back soon, didn't you tell her you were coming? No, I wanted to surprise her.

I'll say! She'll be so happy! Do you plan to stay with us for the holidays? Of course, I came for that very reason. These past years my mother was around and I couldn't leave her alone, but now that she has died. . . . He was looking around as if to ask himself: where have I landed? He didn't seem too thrilled by the mess in our house, by the books scattered all over. Well, sit down then, shall I make you some coffee? But he said no. When's Maria coming back? In a little while, don't worry, she's got so much work to do, she never leaves for very long. And I could already read his mind: if she has so much work to do to financially support you both, why don't you go grocery shopping instead of her? I could have told him that I sleep in and I really don't feel like going shopping as soon as I wake up, and I especially don't like to carry up the bottled water that weighs a ton.

Luckily, just at that moment the door opened and Maria stepped in softly humming a tune. As soon as she saw him, she let out a scream of joy and ran to embrace him, dropping the grocery bags on the floor. How she kissed him, her François! I had never seen them together; whenever he would come, it was to take her quickly away, he never stayed the night, they just left immediately and that was it. Now he will stay with us, he'll sleep with Maria in her bed and I'll be green with envy, where can you find such a handsome man and for free at that!

December 22

The ridiculous one has arrived, though to look at him he's not so ridiculous, the *mon amour*, he's as lovely as the sun, mom is overjoyed and hugs him all the time, she's truly in love, even if in my opinion he could go for a younger girl, a sharper one, funnier, fresher than mom but you don't look a gift horse in the mouth, no . . . maybe that's not the right saying, let's just say, she found him, she took him, and she's keeping him all to herself, lucky woman!

Yesterday Tulù talked to me about his future, which he sees as bleak and hopeless, I'll probably go to Germany, he says, to look for a good job, here nobody respects or helps you, But you haven't even finished school, Tulù! be a little more patient, isn't it too early to emigrate? Well, my brother's gone to England, my cousin Giovanni's in South Africa, his girlfriend, who just got her diploma, is about to join him, do you really think I can have a better future by staying in my own country, I mean, who invests in having a young person study and then kicks him out and away? Well, wait at least until you graduate high school, and then we'll see, maybe we can go live in the countryside and start a farm with lots of cows and lots of chickens and we can sell the calves and the eggs and make cheese, It seems like a silly idea to me, who would take care of the cows and the chickens, you? Why not, don't you think I can do it? I just can't see you, with your moped, your piercings, that dragon on your back, milking the cows, selling the calves at the market on Sunday, feeding the chickens, no, I just don't see you getting up at five o'clock in the morning to clean out the stalls and then rake hay, getting ticks and ants all over yourself, Yeah but Ettore did it, you remember Ettore, who used to go to our school, older than us by a few years? He got his diploma, did a year of Erasmus and then he bought some abandoned land in the countryside for cheap with a loan from his parents, he restored a crumbling farmhouse, bought two cows and a few chicks, every year those cows have a calf, by selling off two calves he bought himself another cow and then another, in the meantime he sells the milk he draws from their udders with an electric sucker, the chicks have grown and had other chicks, now he has about twenty chickens and a beautiful rooster who looks like a parakeet all colored with a crest that shines, he sells the calves off two at a time, in a few years he'll have about a hundred cows and thousands of chickens and he already makes tons of money, how about it, we could do the same, and then besides I'll get myself that dog I've always wanted, I already have a name for it, his name will be Prometheus, my mom says he was a friend of man, in fact the first friend of human beings: she says he stole intelligence and memory from Athena's riches to give them to man, not to mention fire that he stole from Zeus, who as revenge chained him to a rock and sent an eagle there every night to eat his liver, which grew back by day, but at night it was eaten again, my mom knows so many stories, but I like this Prometheus, so if I get a dog that's what I'm calling him. Prometheus.

My grandmother asks me about Tulù, He's fine, *nonna*, but she insists: is he handsome? does he have other girlfriends besides you? what's his hair like: I hope he doesn't lose his hair like your father, who was already bald at thirty, I don't answer her, it bothers me that she has eyes for Tulù. Are you jealous perhaps? she asks, Of course not, *nonna*, it's just that, how can I put this? You are out, out, out of your mind, at your age you should be thinking about the grave not about dance halls, about young men and other stupid crap, As long as I'm alive, I want to have fun, Like Mirandolina? Like Mirandolina, yes, do you have something to say to that? Mirandolina was my age, *nonna*, And I'm as old as I feel: just turned thirty, no more, I'm healthy, I'm fresh, I like to have fun, and I do, what more do you want? when I die, I die, I don't give a fuck, after all when you're underground you don't feel anything and you don't see anything, you just sleep, rest my soul!

December 23

I've sewn a pocket inside my blue jacket. Otherwise, where do I put you, my little tape recorder? I like to take you out when I'm in the bathroom, or when I'm walking down the street. It used to be they would look at me askance: this one's crazy! Not now, because everyone talks to themselves, with that earphone cord that goes across their chest. No one is surprised, even when they laugh out loud, all by themselves or when they make hand gestures shouting like a lunatic because they might be arguing with their spouse.

The beautiful Frenchman has taken up residence at our home and is so polite and clean and neat that you can't find anything to fault him with. He sets the table for lunch and for dinner, then he cleans off the dishes and diligently stacks them in the dishwasher. He insisted that we each tuck our rolled-up cloth napkins in the painted wooden rings that he bought and brought home as a grand gift. Everyone has their own color, purple for me, green for Maria, blue for Lori. For himself, he kept the golden one that sparkles on the tablecloth. He observed, with infinite aplomb, that we eat too fast, that we get up too often from the table, that we drink too much water and too little wine, in short, he's imposing his lifestyle to which we are adapting even if a bit reluctantly. He's the god of love and one simply cannot say no to him.

He disapproved of the dragon on Lori's back, and she in turn, shameless as she is, immediately went and showed it to him by taking off her sweater. He has a way of wrinkling his nose that reminds me of one of those young ladies from a good family from the time when, as a little girl, my parents sent me to a boarding school run by nuns for a few months, and from which I naturally ran away as soon as I had the chance. There's nothing feminine about this love god, but his good manners make him a bit like a snobbish young lady even though he has a well-toned muscular body that surely makes every man he passes on the street green with envy.

Yesterday he insisted on waking up early to take Lori to school with Maria's car. You're generous and kind, said my naive daughter who can't see as far as the tip of her nose. I'd be more on my guard because those two look at each other too much. It's true that I look at him too, how can you not? Let's just say I admire him and look him over with no ambitions of possession, while it seems to me that that crafty Lori fixes her eyes on him with a great desire—and quite obvious at that—to eat him up in one bite. Poor Maria!

The baker was waiting for me, he had put aside some freshly baked bread. Luckily the store was empty and he grabbed me by the arm and took me to the back of the store to kiss me. He held me close, trembling like a little boy. With him, I have to close my eyes because he's not a beauty like François. A conventional charm, that's what Simone has, big hairy wrists, thick eyebrows, a Roman nose, a sweet smile but with a few crooked teeth. I'm fine with his not wanting to have sex. He's impotent, he confessed to me in a moment of frankness. But he likes being wooed, he likes kisses, in fact he told me that for him kisses are the most important thing about love, that he could live on kisses, that the kiss is a gift from God, that he would kiss even the ugliest mouth in the world, as long as it has soft lips and the nice smell of a love-mouth. Another love god? In short, he kept me there for a half hour to talk about the power of the kiss, forgetting all about his customers who were rumbling about in the store. He whispered that when he kisses, his skin turns goosey, that's what he said to me, it gets all prickly and he feels his stomach turn round and he's so happy that he would never stop kissing me, Have you always been impotent? I asked him, were you born that way or did you become so? He looked at me with two beautiful eyes, desperate, and he answered me that when he dreams he has an erection and he cums by himself, but when he has a woman's body in front of him, he doesn't get hard, and there's nothing he can do about it, but when he kisses he flies to paradise and every kiss is a promise of love. I'm not a pervert, though, he insists on saying, he doesn't force himself on anyone, he asks and kisses only if a woman consents. Oh, okay, thanks, of course, no doubt.

He's a strange fellow, my baker, a person to immediately hand over to a psychiatrist. I wonder what he would say, how the psychiatrist would define him. . . . But Simone doesn't feel like he's sick, just a bit inhibited. He lets himself go with me, he knows I understand him and he waits for me every morning to give me bread and a good morning kiss. A long, tasty, and warm kiss, very exciting, despite his leaving me a bit frustrated.

December 24

Holidays are in the air, the city's all decked out, but it's more like a sideshow than anything else: all the trees are loaded with lights, poor trunks that must feel prickly from all those lights, not even a moment of rest during the night, a bit of darkness to sleep, and what about the birds that are confused and edgy because of all this light and bulbs that occupy the branches for their nests, where do those birds go?

The beautiful François takes it easy; like *nonna* he sleeps in the morning, while mom goes food shopping, she comes back with newspapers, loaded down by the mineral water, exotic fruit, he like mangoes and avocados, besides I'd like to know why a fruit is called an advocate, it obviously doesn't know the law, it doesn't go to trial, Give me a couple pounds of advocates! With toga or without? No, I say, inside a plastic bag, and the lovely François eats and eats, always on the edge of his seat, on the edge of his plate, off the tip of his fork, he's well-mannered and very precise, he insists the tablecloth be cleaned and ironed, that the silverware be placed properly, fork on the left, knife on the right, dessert spoon on top and even the plates must be ceramic, heaven forbid they should be plastic, real glassware and fortunately mom knew it and she quickly organized everything, heaven forbid we should use paper napkins, they must be cotton and freshly pressed each time, you don't throw them away after one use, you wash and iron them and who does that? and the wine must be a good wine, preferably French, not our awful wine that comes in a carton, he tastes and nods yes or no, but it's not cheap and mom racks up debts to buy the French wine that he likes, mama Maria will soon grow a halo and even wings, but she will never fly away, because she's a housewife, and one who always has her nose stuck in a book and thinks that to fly away like Peter Pan is vulgar and cowardly, she's always there at the stake, working like a jackass, he however is kind, always available, he even helps set the table, cut the bread, take out the water from the fridge, prepare the fruit and that's it, if he weren't so good-looking you wouldn't forgive him, but every movement he makes is so soft, so elegant that your mouth drops open just to look at him.

December 25

Maria seems quite restless, I see her breathlessly running about, trying to juggle the translation that she's been struggling to finish after François's arrival, the good stuff to cook for Christmas dinner, the gifts to buy and wrap, the long slumbers of her love who seems to be sleep deprived, the tantrums thrown by Lori who races off in the morning on her moped and you never really know if she ever goes to school and when she'll be back, and if you say anything to her, she strikes back like a viper. I don't think that Tulù is leading her on the right path, I think he was the one who convinced her to get that dragon tattoo on her back. He's covered in flowers, moons, skulls, but who knows what other secrets he has, you never know. How does he manage to live by himself in an apartment in the city, when he's still going to school? Are his parents so rich they can afford a place in a luxury building?

And in these four walls, there is me who irritates her with my irony, I know, I feel bad because I see Maria tired and out of breath, but the elf in my head always wants to come out of my mouth in the form of mischievous words and doesn't want to hear anything about keeping still in its nest.

Not writing letters anymore is as if she's lost the equilibrium of her day. Without letters to write she's forced to dedicate herself only to the translations and Flaubert follows her around all day long with his contradictions. François is becoming lazier and lazier and handsomer, resplendent actually, like a Saint Michael ready to pierce the dragon. There's something powerful in his svelte and lanky body, something aflame and sacred in those eyes whose color I still haven't figured out, sometimes I think they're neutral and reflect the color of what he's wearing: dark blue like a calm and welcoming sea, gray and stormy when he's alarmed, violet like flower juice in a clear glass when he's thinking of love and smiles contentedly.

Maria is certainly lucky, after an irresponsible husband who left this life when Lori was just four years old, leaving her poor and alone, she's lucky to have found this divine gift. Even if he doesn't shine with wealth and munificence, he seems perfect, the magnificent François: he speaks slowly in polished Italian, with a barely discernible French accent, smiles like an angel, moves like a tango dancer, helps set and clear off the table, carries up the case of mineral water from the store, leaves the bathroom clean without a trace of hair, even when he shaves, goes out often on his own and comes back with a book in his hand. He says he likes to go for walks. He wears comfortable, soft, elegant shoes that look like they'd been made just for him, for long, elastic feet. He doesn't wear socks, now and then his bare ankles protrude under his pants and they are white and hairless, they express something in contrast to that muscular body: an awkward timidity and perhaps a great need for protection. It's quite strange, though, that he doesn't wear hosiery or socks. And yet his feet never smell when he takes his shoes off. He seems to have been born with them already glued to his feet, comfortable and perfect for walking several inches off the ground like a new Hermes with wings on his ankles, as a matter of fact he makes no noise, he's a prince with wings, beautiful and in love.

December 26

The best gift: a puppy from the shelter, because we have to save the poor, abandoned dogs, as my mom says, a little chubby, hairy sausage, with a black muzzle that sticks out from the fur that covers almost all of its sly, sharp eyes, it's now wagging merrily about the house, happy because someone took it out of that horrible cage and pets it and smothers it with pampering and food, who gave it to me? it's unbelievable, but it was beautiful François himself who found out what I wanted from mom and he even paid to liberate it from the pound and brought it to be washed and combed, I wasn't expecting it when he put it in my arms yesterday saying I know you really wanted one so here's your gift from me, I jumped for joy, that man certainly knows how to win people over. What will you do when you go out? my mom asks, but today I've already found a way of bringing it with me by attaching a basket behind the seat of my moped: I stuffed it in there and it was radiant and didn't even try to get out, but it let itself be carried away with its ears to the wind, his name's Prometheus and no bird is going to eat his liver, that I can guarantee, the vet says he's female but I've already given him a masculine name, I don't like Promethea, it will be Prometheus even if it is a girl, she runs, she plays, she already recognizes me as soon as I call her, and she jumps on my lap and licks my ears when I hold her in my arms, she's a cheerful little thing, she must be more or less five months old, but she acts like an adult, she seems to know that her fate was a prison and her gratitude has no limits, she knows instinctively when I want her to play or when I want her to be still, she crouches under the table and sleeps peacefully, sometimes placing her little head on my feet.

December 30

Prometheus has arrived, that's what Lori decided to call the puppy that François gave her for Christmas. A very excited little pup that jumps and licks and chews on everything that's within the reach of her muzzle, irresistible because of its cheerfulness but also very unwieldy. Who's going to take it out? For now Lori doesn't leave it for a moment, when she decides to go out, she scoops it up and puts it in a basket attached to her moped. The puppy crouches down and is quiet for hours, it already understands everything Lori says and it wags its tail like nobody's business at whatever it is told to do. It's a mix of a poodle and another stray dog, I'm guessing, apparently someone threw it in the trash bin, was taken out by someone else who brought it to the city pound and that's when it was put in a cage. It's always running around; luckily it doesn't bark very much and it tries to understand instinctively whatever it is that whoever is around it needs. The strategies of a stray dog that wants to quickly learn survival techniques. You can't help but like it. It looks like a male dog to me but Lori brought it to a vet who says it's a female and so it should be called Promethea, a more incongruous name one could not imagine, but it comes from that nose-stuck-in-a-book daughter of mine, Maria, who when given the chance, turns to the Greek myths to guide her literary vision.

It looks like she's almost finished with her Flaubert, she's revising it to hand it over before New Year's, she announced publicly, showing the world the printed pages written on the computer. In the meantime, she's getting ready to take off with François, right after the holidays, for Holland, who knows why, it's such an insipid country, the yearnings of exoticism are over, it seems like all the most beautiful countries are off limits because of the terrorism that's threatening anyone who cultivates the pleasure of wanderlust to foreign lands. Tourism is focusing on old Europe: our Venice is exploding because of the many shoes that stomp its *calli*, because of the shit that travelers deposit in our toilets. One never realizes that every tourist who brings in money also brings in shit and pee that run off into our sewers that then end up in the sea or the river making them smelly and sterile.

There's news on the bakery front: Simone has found a girlfriend and as a result he no longer grabs me by the arm to the back of the store. I asked him if he managed penetration with this Giusy and he answered enigmatically: almost. What do you mean almost? But he didn't answer me, he just smiled mysteriously. He then showed me a photo of Giusy who's as white as a corpse, very skinny and wearing glasses that cover half her face. I want to get married, he said, and have kids and she's the only one who calms my nerves, with her it's like making love to myself, that's why I think I can manage to do it, he whispered in my ear, but I will miss your kisses, Gesuina. I wonder if I'll miss them too. But will you come with me once in a while to the back of the store for a stolen kiss? He made me laugh with that sly face of a fox who has spotted a fat chicken. We'll see, I answered, and we will really see what my senses, ever unpredictable and unexpected, will tell me.

François of course would be ideal for kissing, but he seems like the most faithful man in the world and now it looks like he's dedicating all his attention toward Prometheus: he sets her on his lap, he allows her to lick his face and he laughs happily with the gift that he seems to have given himself rather than to the young daughter of the woman he loves. They'll be leaving for the Netherlands, he and Maria, and they're already organizing the trip into the midst of the watery lands of a country full of surprises. They'll go to Amsterdam to see the Van Gogh museum, they'll go to Utrecht to see the remains of the Roman fortification, the *castellum* that dates back to 47 A.D., François proudly said, they'll visit the famous cathedral tower, they'll push on all the way to Den Helder to the extreme North Country to see the white Scottish cliffs on the sea. By dint of talking about it even I've learned so much about Holland that I'm just about ready for the trip myself. And how about Bruegel? says Maria, because she has a thing for Bruegel the Elder and his narrative tapestries that tell stories about the peasant feasts, the dances, and the fairs of a teeming and joyous world, even if mortified and lice infested.

Yes, of course, Simone is right. I do feel nostalgic for his kisses. I long for something, not only the warmth of his lips but the steady flow of his theories on kisses that upset the senses and carry well-being and peace to the heart and soul. I hear his voice in my ear exalting the beauty of kisses, the sweetness of kisses, the delirious softness of kisses. But as an end unto themselves. One does not go beyond them, he says: usually kisses are an antipasto to more hearty and nutritious foods, but for him, no, he theorizes that kisses represent the antipasto, the main course, the side dishes of an imaginary love meal, and perhaps he's right. One can get full on kisses alone, with kisses one can fatten up one's sensual imagination and with kisses one can reach exhaustion. But how will you get those kisses with the very skinny and cadaver-like Giusy? I asked sincerely worried. Well, I'm not marrying her for the kisses but because I want a child. Have you wanted a child for a while? For years, I don't know why but I crave it, I can already envision him walking beside me, in his little shorts, the softness of his little hand in mine, and I feel happy. Kisses and a kid, you're really odd, I say. And he smiles. If I could have a kid with just kisses, I'd sign on immediately. Have you ever had sex with Giusy, I asked him. Never, was his reply. Never never? Never never, Gesuina, I don't like sex unto itself, I don't like copulation, it's ordinary, predictable and fast, it ends quickly and doesn't provide any intimate rewards, how can you compare it to kisses? Well, then, how will you ever have a child? It'll happen sooner or later, we'll go all the way, but only to bake up a son, he answered. I have to admit that he has infected me, his theory on kissing as the only recourse to carnal love convinces me and I make it my own: okay, so goodbye, Simone, I leave you to your cadaver-like Giusy who doesn't know how to kiss but probably knows how to have a kid without even cumming, like the Madonna, by parthenogenesis, or with the help of some servile bread maker who works on call in your bakery.

January 15

Mom and François have left for Holland, the house seems empty, luckily there's Prometheus, the one who thinks first, I like the idea of thinking first, it's pretty cool, something I don't know how to do, that's why I like it, mom says I'm crazy, that a dog can't be called Prometheus, that one who thinks before speaking or acting is a demigod, that's why Zeus sent an eagle to him every day to peck at his liver that would grow back at night and in the morning would end up in that ugly bird's beak, maybe mom's right, too many literary inferences, but when a name gets into a body it stays there forever. I don't understand why but I just can't help but think of my dog as Prometheus, even if it's a female, all furry, with a moist muzzle, even if there's nothing heroic or powerful about her, but she's tiny and she does nothing but ingratiate herself with people whimpering and putting on a kind of smile that in reality is a grin, but she's here now, her name is Prometheus and we love each other, do secrets have a reason for staying secret? I ask myself, the fear of espionage transforms secrets into stupid secrets, I am a secret or is it that my body is carrying a secret that I can't utter? the secret is racing but I cannot have it gallop onto the pages because it would become a thought and I don't want to think of the future, it terrifies me, I want to die but without dying, I want to live but without knowing it, I want to fly but with my feet on the ground, I want I want, I am so messed up by an impossible desire, I don't believe in kisses, unlike my *nonna* who believes only in those and she talks to me about them as if they were gems, can one be nurtured by gems no matter how precious? the secret will remain secret because that's what my body wants, a body that lives on unknown impulses and happy departures and joys conquered without even knowing it, for now I limit myself to racing with my Prometheus along the city streets, Tulù was generous: he's allergic to dogs, but nevertheless he welcomed her into his home, with a few caveats, but he lets me bring her with me when I go to his house, we close her up in the kitchen while we do our homework or make love without thinking of anything, she keeps still, she doesn't bark or anything, she crouches under the table and sleeps until she hears me say Prometheus let's go! and then leaps into the air like a jumping spider and grabs the leash as if to say that he, or rather she, is ready and we can go.

January 26

There's something up with Lori. Sometimes she seems depressed, as if inhabited by dark and solemn thoughts, other times she exudes sparks of life that make her laugh senselessly. Was it perhaps Prometheus that changed her in this way by overwhelming her monotonous life? She certainly doesn't leave her for a moment and contrary to what Maria was saying, she takes care of her with sweet patience: she prepares her meals of boiled fish or steamed ground meat, mixed with boiled rice and dressed with olive oil. She takes her out in the morning and in the afternoon, for long walks from which they both come back exhausted and they throw themselves down, Lori on her bed and the dog on the rug on the floor.

I asked her why she's so angry, but she didn't answer me. It's like she's mad at the whole world but at other times she smothers me with kisses and says, You'll see, *nonna*, we're going to make it. Make what? I don't get it, she's mysterious, like she's keeping a secret: but what? Maria wrote from Utrecht. She says it's cold and raining, but that the Dutch cities are beautiful, and that they often go by boat from one city to the next following the contorted and unpredictable lines of the canals. The Dutch are extraordinary, she writes, and they've already made friends with other couples. It may be, but I don't much believe in travel friendships. They last as long as the movements here and there and then they dry up like water in the sun.

I've not given up the habit of going to the bakery to get fresh bread. Simone smiles at me allusively. More than once he's pulled me by the arm toward the back of the store for a quick stolen kiss. He still has that nice smell of flour, yeast, and butter. I don't know if they add butter to their bread, they probably use it for the pastries that they now bake every hour given their success, but his lips carry the sweet and soft flavor of butter fused with cinnamon.

And how is Giusy? I asked just to say something. Good, she's good, she's pregnant and I'll be marrying her soon. So you managed after all? Yah, I don't know how, Gesuina, but I managed to do it and now we'll have a kid and I'll be a happy father. A happy father who seeks kisses outside his family, I said just to provoke him, but he smiles slyly and squeezes my arm with a gesture of solidarity and of complicity. We'll just have our little secret and that's all. And what if I should find another baker who loves kisses as much as you do? I'd suffer, but I'd understand, I'm not so crazy as to expect what I myself don't give: fidelity. Do what you like, but don't tell me, I'd feel really bad. Does that mean you have feelings for me? I asked, almost moved by his speech. I'm crazy about you, he answered asking for another kiss and then another. I whispered in his ear a famous poem by Catullus that I had once recited aloud in a little theater on a long-ago Christmas Eve: *Give me a thousand kisses and then a hundred more, / then another thousand, and again a hundred more, / and then without stopping another thousand, / and again a hundred, and / when we will have given many thousands of them / we will hide them / so that no evil can look with scorn upon us / knowing that we had given each other so many kisses.*

The poem brought to mind my brief career as an actress and how I did not like being on stage, I felt awkward and out of place even though that smell of dust and old curtains fascinated me. It was the audience that frightened me: those dolled-up bodies in front of me in the darkness intimidated me. I love squishy bodies, I love them timid and lost, I love when they undress a little to let me see a wound, an overgrown mole, they are trusting bodies, bodies that are asking for help, that are not demanding, but that hide their own nakedness and would like the world to swallow them up before showing their hidden sores. Those are the bodies I love and that's why I wanted to be a doctor. But everyone was against it: a woman doctor, and who would ever go to you for medical help? maybe a pediatrician, perhaps, but I don't have the patience for children, I don't understand them and I get agitated when they start to cry, I'm not good with them, and besides kids don't know how to kiss, they slobber your face with saliva and they might even pee all over you.

But let's return to that odd fellow named Simone whom I've almost grown fond of, I may even love him and he makes me happy, it seems incredible that he interests me, me who plays the cynic who doesn't believe in affection. The power of stolen kisses, secret kisses, of betrayal. Another and yet another, Simone, long live kisses!

January 26

Dear Mom and Lori,

It's now very clear to me that to understand Holland it is absolutely necessary to pass through Van Gogh's canvases. These portraits of peasants with stunned faces, crumpled hoods on their heads, clogs on their feet tell age-old stories of hard work and calluses, little to eat and dampness that enters into their bones and deforms them. The peasant with a pipe in his mouth and a red kerchief on his neck has an aspect that is so overcome by fatigue that he seems to almost slip into a zone of the unhuman. With an unkind eye the painter observes the potato eaters holed up in a dark room, but then you realize that it is merely a factual gaze: men and women with a tired and amused air, closed up in a place with dark walls, sit around a table illuminated by an oil lamp hung from the ceiling lighting up certain features of their faces and hands: one is grabbing a teapot, another a cup of hot tea, another some fabric to be mended.

Immediately after, the tale continues with the vision of two women peasants who are tilling the soil, portrayed backlit in a hostile environment, bent over clods of earth, their skirts swollen around their hips. Next to them are many still lifes that show humble foodstuffs: apples, squash, onions, cabbage. You cannot imagine on how many canvases our Vincent paints potatoes as if he had seen them for the first time only as an adult and with a bewildered eye: the most useful but also the most mistreated among vegetables. One, two, three paintings tell the story of the potatoes with sharp attention, drawing the eye ever closer to the tubers. Thrown into white and yellow bowls, spread out on a blackish cloth, each painted one by one with maniacal concentration: a veritable obsession, this of the potatoes, covered with holes, lopsided and scorned bumps, potatoes that have suffered from hunger, they too, in this arid and lowly land. Van Gogh could not have better depicted the poverty of a peasant folk who secured their future by digging up those lumpy vegetables with lumpy hands.

I stopped for a long time in front of the portrait of a prostitute who has nothing sensual about her: she is wearing a bluish shirt and a thin metal necklace with a cross hanging from it. The girl is young but a bit plump, her hair is gathered in a bun on the nape of her neck, on her ears hang two small pearls, probably bought after days of amorous pretenses. To put up with a strange body that you do not know and likely despise, you must quiet your senses, don't you think? you have to deaden your stomach, you have to anesthetize it; and the girl in the painting seems to know this simple and age-old art, the art of destitute women who have as their only wealth their welcoming, alluring body. What is surprising is the tenacity, the tender coolness with which Van Gogh describes the Holland of his times, poor, belabored, divided into two very distinct societies: the poor on one side, who at thirty were already old, had rotted teeth, wrinkled faces, legs swollen by arthrosis, and on the other side, the rich, who dressed in satin and silk, wore wigs or colored feathers in their hair, they, too, with rotting teeth, though they turned to the barber-surgeon to have them removed.

Even the city women do not appear much healthier or even more sensual than the peasant women in wooden clogs: they are a bit hunched over and rather ugly, but full of pride, and they have a decisive and proudful sense of self written on their faces. The young madame of the Café Le Tambourin is wearing a red hat on her head that looks like a giant cockscomb. She is not smiling and seems immersed in her own thoughts. The thing that moves me is the absolute lack of exposed feelings: no compassion, solidarity, social indignation, but a calm and painful observation of reality. And in the end a simple and linear capacity to identify oneself with the observed figure, be it a peasant woman, a bourgeois woman, a prostitute, or a street urchin.

A figure that frequently reoccurs is that of the postman of Arles, Joseph Roulin: a man with large, deformed hands, squeezed into a blue uniform with gold buttons and a beard that in the various paintings grows longer and more elaborate. They say that the postman was a frequent visitor to the Van Gogh home, because we see him seated on one of those famous wicker chairs that the young Vincent would use when he painted in his humble home in Arles. It is as if he were drawn with the same dreamy hand with which he signs his self-portraits, even the one with the bandage on the ear he cut off. As he gets older and his hand becomes more ungovernable and shakier, his landscapes become shocked and distorted, as if narrated by one who is drugged and sees everything hazy and transformed: fields of grain over which blows a furious and arcane wind; clouds that are transformed into flying cabbageheads, and lights that pierce through the leaden fabric of a merciless sky. The brush races breathlessly, biting and lyrical at the same time, as if pursued by an agony without remedy.

I'm sorry, I have probably bored you with my impressions, but I really could not peel my eyes from my beloved

Vincent and from his canvases that speak with such vehemence to the imagination of who is watching. I have not even asked how you are doing. François and I are in great form, happy to be together while touring these lands so dangerously immersed in the waters of a sea that seems to be a friend but that at times transforms itself into an enemy that attacks and tends to invade and swallow up all that lies in front of it.

How is dear Prometheus, or rather dear Promethea? Who takes her out now that François is no longer in the house? I hope Lori plops her in the basket and takes her around on her moped as she was doing at first.

Sending you my hugs, along with François. Tomorrow we are going to visit the home of Anne Frank. I will tell you all about it afterward.

Till then,
Maria

February 2

Mom wrote from her Netherlands, as happy as a lark and as blind as a dormouse, she observes the beloved paintings with an attentive eye, but besides the paintings, mommy dearest, what is there for you? is it possible that you see only what is fake and you don't understand what is happening under your nose, in your own house? is it possible that you don't see how everything is crumbling and wasting away while you hug and kiss your man in a distant Holland, lost in the Van Gogh paintings, but blind to the rest?

Prometheus vomited all day yesterday, I had to take her to the vet, he says she must have eaten something off the street that had gone bad, now she's on a strict diet and detox injections, which she tolerates with blessed patience, *nonna* doesn't help me at all, she says that dogs make her yawn and that's all, though it's not true because when I'm not around she keeps the dog on her lap, she caresses and cuddles her while recording her nonsense on her little pocket tape recorder, I surprised her one morning when I came home earlier than usual, I don't know what's happened with Simone the baker because she now buys bread someplace else, and she's moved on to another totally platonic relationship with a certain Filippo whose photo she showed me, a nice-looking man with a foolish air, high cheekbones, wide forehead and a very fleshy mouth. *Nonna* don't trust him, I told her, you know there are image thieves, it's not a given that the photo is really the person who's writing you, it could be an ugly sleazy pig who, once he's managed to make a fool of you, will ask you for some money and you'll give it to him because you're foolish and you fall into love traps like a silly girl, she burst out laughing, I don't understand why you're such a pessimist, Lori, not only did he send me his picture, but his address and a picture of his family, too. He even has a family, this Filippo of yours? Yes, a wife and two daughters, but he says they're not enough and he needs someone intelligent with whom to communicate, And this intelligent someone would be you, *nonna*? Why? do I seem stupid to you? In matters of love, yes, you're one who believes everything and falls into every trap like a dummy. I'm more careful than you think, I know what I'm doing and I don't allow anyone to fool me, I keep my guard up, no one takes me by the nose, I hope so for your sake, *nonna*, I told her, but she doesn't listen to me, she goes straight on her path of a sixty-year-old in love with love and kisses, I just hope she doesn't allow these internet freaks to rob her of too much money, How I would like to have a grandmother like everyone else, one who thinks only of her grandchildren and their future! I said, and she just laughed and shrugged.

February 10

I want a normal grandmother, my granddaughter says to make me feel guilty. A totally dedicated grandmother, willing to make sacrifices, that's what you want, dear Lori, but that you will never have, because I'm a free person and not a family institution. Such demands! Can you be more egotistical? The other one, my daughter, is not coming home at this point, all she does is galivant around the many realities of her Holland with the man she loves, and the two of us here, burning pans, flooding the bathroom: without her everything's falling apart here. Especially since that pest Promethea arrived; it's even sick now and soils all over the place with her shit and vomit.

Meanwhile, Simone has become more insistent. What does this man want, who in the interim went and got himself married, all he ever talks about is his desire to have a child and at the same time he doesn't want to lose his kisses, about which he constantly theorizes. The latest is that his wife, Giusy, isn't even pregnant, he had said so just to show off but the long-awaited son is nowhere to be seen, not even close. In the meantime, I have an outlet with Filippo, who already has kids and who has a stable relationship of reciprocal tolerance with his wife and there's no talk of kisses except in writing. Even words can be sensual, just like kisses, and we write to each other obsessively and love each other without ever having seen each other, just by a parallel vocation. An affectionate man, sensitive, perhaps not very cultured, actually, let's just say he's an ignoramus, when I told him about Mirandolina he asked me, Who's this

Mirandolina, a friend of yours? I don't think he's ever set foot in a theater in his life. He works in coffee: he travels to Latin America to buy coffee and resells it on the Italian market. When he writes to me, I smell the aroma of coffee that engulfs him. He tells me about so many blends of coffee, arabica that comes from Africa and has less caffeine, *Coffea arabica* he calls it, and then there's *Coffea robusta* or *Coffea canephora* that also comes from Africa but it is not cultivated on the plateau and contains more caffeine. And let's not forget the *Coffea liberica* blend, that comes from Liberia, and *Coffea racemosa* from Cameroon.

The word *coffee*, he tells me (he knows everything about coffee but very little about theater or music) comes from the word *qahwa* which the Turks then transformed into *kahve*, which finally became coffee for us. They say it has medicinal qualities, even Muḥammad was cured of the flu by drinking huge cups of coffee, that's what he tells me, happy to be able to teach me things of which I was completely unaware. He likes to surprise me with his knowledge about coffee. He knows everything about its origins, about where it's produced in the world, about how many bags circulate on the international market and he even knows the history of the holy liquid. The English were the first to make it a national beverage, in every village of the 1700s there was a coffee-house, he explains haughtily, and you should know that only at the end of the eighteenth century was the African coffee plant brought to Latin America and there it rapidly spread.

The best blend according to Artusi? Two hundred and fifty grams of Puerto Rico, 100 grams of San Domingo and 150 grams of mocha. The most sought after in the world, the *kopi luwak*, produced in Indonesia and so on: long story short, he fills my head with his endless knowledge of a caffeine maniac and I find that rather sweet because he places in that coffee his future, his passion and even his sensuality. He told me that in Al Hudaydah, the homeland of mocha, while he was walking around with his pockets full of coffee samples to test, he came upon some prisoners with an iron ball and chain attached to their ankles. And why was that? They are so poor that they don't have any prisons and so they set prisoners free, barefoot, but attached to a heavy iron ball that they barely manage to drag along, and they live on alms because they no longer have a home or someone to give them food to eat: very odd, don't you think?

February 15

My dearly beloved Gesuina and Lori,

It is raining here, hail rather, no, ice balls are flying about breaking through umbrellas and they accumulate in the street sending many people head over heels, both the old and the very young. I am very careful and have never fallen, but you know who has fallen instead? François, that's right, the elegant, lanky athlete François, who walks without ever looking down, almost went flying. He slipped and fell down hard resulting in a huge fist-sized bruise on his right leg. Fortunately, he did not break anything and when he got back up, we started to laugh, so hard that we were about to fall down again, the two of us. To shake it off and warm ourselves up, we went into a café and ordered a nice hot toddy.

The other day we visited the home of Anne Frank, the girl with the diary I read with such fervor as a teenager. But we were disappointed because they made a museum out of it, complete with entrance fee, postcards, T-shirts with her name, and a guide who recounts her story. The photographs that cover the walls are done well, though, along with the films that continually project a Holland under Nazi rule, the search of the homes, the roundup of the Jews who were hauled into freight trains locked with iron bolts and then brought to Auschwitz or Bergen-Belsen. As happened to poor Anne, who in her sweet diary describes how she lived hidden next to noisy and careless neighbors, in forced silence, always waiting with trepidation for the only person who knew of the hiding place to bring them enough food to survive. Without that woman and that food they would have died of starvation in the three small rooms concealed behind a wall of books. But every day it became more and more difficult to remain quiet, the anxiety grew, the living arrangements became strained, the constant fights over trivial matters such as one less or one more glass of water, a wet rag left by chance on a chair, a piece of bread missing from the cupboard, a book claimed by two readers. Someone, though, and it seems it was a housemaid particularly loyal to the regime, will become aware of the family and will serve as spy. They will come to get them one early morning and will take them all to Bergen-Belsen in Lower Saxony. There Anne Frank will find herself locked in a shed with bunk beds and without a mattress or bed linens, with only a filthy blanket invaded by lice, amid common criminals, Jews, political prisoners, Gypsies, Jehovah's Witnesses, and homosexuals, separated from her parents and those with whom she had shared the hideaway.

From that moment on we know nothing more of little Anne Frank. It is assumed she was taken to the gas chamber shortly after her parents, after her sister Margot and her neighbors. In the first months of 1943 they say fifty thousand people had already died in that camp. Among those Anne Frank, petite, dark haired, with a kind and innocent smile, and eyes shining with the desire to love. Only her father survived and, it seems, he was the one who wanted to publish her diary and have it read by the whole world so that no one should forget what happened under the Nazis during the last war.

February 20

Hello, hello . . . I just changed the batteries, why are you so slow to turn on, you darn thing? Hello, hello, hello, yes, yes, well? are we on? are we working? Ah, finally! now you seem to be working, I was about to throw you in the trash . . . so let's pick up the conversation where we left off: my daughter, Maria, now writes to us, now that she has her beloved François next to her, the habit of writing letters has not abandoned her, she sends us letters, we who have stayed at home and have to do everything by ourselves, grocery shopping, cooking, washing the dishes, making the beds, paying the bills, in short a heap of hassles . . . when are you two coming back, darn it, it's been almost two months that you've been away. How has the financial officer François Colin managed to take such a long vacation? He says that he's accumulated so many days over the years that he now has exactly two months at his disposal. Doesn't he realize that Maria must continue her translation work and that her staying away so long leaves us in the lurch? Besides that, the dog had a bout of diarrhea and messed up the house. But I refused to clean it up. You wanted a dog? Now you clean up after it! And Lori did, but not without a fair amount of grumbling. I think she's sorry she kept it, even if she can't do without it, at this point, Prometheus or Promethea—damn if I know which—sleeps on her bed and eats at the table with her.

Simone the baker sends me a ton of WhatsApp messages where he says he misses my kisses, then he tells me that his wife can't procreate, she can't get pregnant, while he does his best, but in my opinion his impotence has never healed despite the idea of making love to himself, as he explained to me to justify his choice of that bespectacled corpse of a girl who is supposed to become the mother of his children. I'm almost glad, even though it's vile to wish ill on others.

The relationship with Filippo, on the other hand, is moving along magnificently. He continually writes to me, he sends me pictures of him setting up the Christmas tree, of his two daughters who help him hang these beautiful red baubles on the fake fir. He tells me he lives with his wife but they haven't made love in years, two spouses separated under one roof, though I don't really believe him, but I answer him anyway because it's part of the game and I love to play, even when there's a risk. Filippo, who is certainly not as handsome as François, nor does he have Simone's rounded lips and sweet smile, writes to say that he wants to meet me, but I pull back, I prefer clandestine play. His words weigh in with a subtle and intense pleasure that when I open one of his emails, I get goose bumps. Is it love? Is it desire? I honestly don't know what it is, but it's a lively emotion that slithers up my spine. Who was that friend of mine, I don't remember, who was a fanatic of exotic religions who told me about the kundalini serpent, coiled up at the bottom of one's spine? Only when it wakes up and gets excited, it begins to unwind, climbing up one's back until, with its bifurcated tongue, it blows a warm and potent breath right at the base of your brain.

February 21

My dear sweet Lori and Gesuina,

We are preparing our suitcases for our return. And I am saddened, even if I will be happy to see you again. I have even bought a few tulip bulbs because these flowers of the most unbelievable colors are beautiful and I think they will do just fine on our north-facing balcony.

The symbol of this difficult land, but also very much attuned to unexpected happiness, is indeed the tulip. A strange flower that seems to be created in an oven, made of a delicate and fine ceramic, with something both sparkling and metallic, a flower of splendid colors but no perfume. Why, I ask myself, have the Dutch chosen this strange and impassive flower as a symbol of their country? Where was it born?

I have read that the tulip originated in Turkey and that it was brought to Europe in 1554 by a Flemish ambassador who gifted a few seeds to the expat French botanist Carolus Clusius, who in turn planted them in the fertile grounds of his adopted country and it immediately became popular. The name *tulip*, I have read further, comes from the Turkish *tullband*, which means "turban," curious, don't you think? a flower so Nordic that comes from an Orient that faces the south. Then the Romantics invented the legend that the tulip was born from the drops of blood of a young man, victim of suicide for love. A hotel leaflet states that a red tulip expresses a declaration of love, a speckled one gallantry, and a violet one represents the modesty of the one who receives and the one who gives. I simply couldn't help but buy a few bulbs to bring back home.

We are returning on Monday by plane. We have already arranged for a taxi to take us home by dinnertime.

See you very soon, with my love,

Maria

February 22

What'll I do, I'd like to know how I'll manage to spit it out, mom'll die from it, I already know that, *nonna* will revile me, I could just keep quiet, I could just take care of it on my own, but can secrets stay secrets forever? can they grow inside of us like tiny bonsai plants and never reveal themselves to the world? I guess not, the only person I can talk to about it is *nonna*, and she certainly will understand me, she's not a moralist and knows what love's all about, I'll talk to her, but when? the lovebirds are coming back on Monday and I'll have to decide.

February 23

An incredible and crazy piece of news: Lori is pregnant. No one could possibly figure out by whom. I'm the only one who knows though, after having bombarded her with questions, she finally gave in. The father is François, who doesn't know. I had guessed it, I have a very fine sense of smell, and I smelled something fishy but I didn't want to believe it and here she is, little Lori pregnant by the man adored by her mother, the beautiful flirty François who, while continuing to call Maria *mon amour*, continuing to treat her as a most loved companion, goes and surreptitiously knocks up her seventeen-year-old daughter. But the problem is how to tell Maria who is normally in the clouds with her Flaubert; it could be lethal news for her.

Nonna, what do you say, I could have an abortion and we won't say anything to anyone?

I don't think it's a good idea, after all a baby would be a nice addition to this household.

But how can I possibly tell mom?

François could tell her, he's the one responsible for this disastrous betrayal.

Mom will die from this and I don't want to kill her, *nonna*, I mean we did it only once and in a hurry, without love, I swear, I've always liked François but I didn't want to steal him from mom, all I wanted to do is clutch that beautiful body, I really had a craving for it, and at a certain point I think even he felt the urge, because all it took was one look to understand each other's desire.

Don't lie, you did everything you could to take him away, but I thought you wouldn't have succeeded, I considered François a faithful lover, but boy was I wrong, and with his beloved's daughter that's really serious stuff, and now that you're pregnant it's even more serious.

February 28

Nonna says that I shouldn't have an abortion, but the very idea of wounding mom makes me vomit, I really don't know how it happened, I never in a million years thought I'd end up pregnant, we did it just one time and there was no love involved, as I explained to *nonna*, but she says it's not true, that I tricked him because I liked beautiful François, no in fact, she says I wanted to steal him away from mom to spite her, but that's not true, why would I have wanted to do something like that? I only wanted to taste him as one wants to taste a wonderful ripe fruit that's under your nose for so long and makes you salivate, all I wanted to do was bite into that sweet pulp and then put it back, unfortunately, that bite took up life in my womb instead and now I'm in big trouble, Don't you see that you have an edible idea of love, you're really contemptible, you shouldn't have done this to your mother, there are so many good-looking boys around, why dip into Maria's lover? *Nonna*, I swear, I wasn't thinking, it just happened, the attraction, the desire, I tell you, we looked straight at each other and decided to do it. That's all, and where did you do it, poor excuse of a granddaughter? Well, Tulù was traveling and he left me the keys to his place, so I brought him there and we had sex on his bed where I normally do it with Tulù, I should tell him about the baby, too, and make him believe that he's the father and that would solve everything, what do you say, *nonna*, Tulù wouldn't suspect anything, and François would certainly not call me out. But why didn't you use a condom? It doesn't cost much. We didn't think of it *nonna*, it all happened so suddenly, without my even wanting to, maybe even he didn't want to, only our bodies wanted to, but I know for sure that he loves mom and not me, and that's why I wouldn't want to ruin everything by telling her about this mess, what if I tell her Tulù's the father and maybe I even marry him? I don't know if he'll agree to that, probably not, the other day he was telling me he wants to go to Germany after high school graduation to look for a job, go figure if he'll want to be stuck around here with an unwanted child, All subterfuges, my child, are uncovered sooner or later, maybe even years later, but the shock for your mother would be even more terrible: twice deceived . . . and besides, aren't you thinking of the deception to Tulù who has nothing to do with all this and what about the poor child who isn't even born yet and will already enter this world in a web of lies? You're right, *nonna*, but I really don't know how to tell her, couldn't you tell her? No, you're the one who created this mess and you're the one who has to tell her, take the bull by the horns and confess everything to her.

March 2

Mom's back with her François all tanned and more handsome than ever, they were holding hands when they walked through the door, placed their luggage on the floor, I bought tulip bulbs, mom immediately said hugging me, and handmade wooden clogs, I gave her a big hug back and kissed her, François seemed a little embarrassed, but oblivious to everything; he hugged me too as if nothing had happened, this morning there was a big discussion with *nonna* about the body and its yearnings, I say the body takes and does what it wants and she contends instead that the body is controlled by the brain. Cravings are held back, my soul, remember, if you let yourself be led by those you are an animal and that's to say that even animals often restrain from certain cravings by a societal and herd instinct that belongs to both animal and human, do you know what sublimation means? and to think that they taught us women, in fact they forced us, obligated us to know this important word, sublimation, What does it mean, *nonna*? It means that one must learn to transform the most natural instincts into generous thoughts, and only by learning, reflection, study, the habit of control, yes even a strong control over one's own instincts, all this teaches you to transform yourself into a conscientious and decent person, You're playing the moralist now, *nonna*? What are you talking about, a moralist! Do you know what it means to be aware? It means to know the consequences of your own actions, if you had practiced a bit of awareness and of sublimation you would not be in this mess now . . . I'm afraid that

she's absolutely right, my duplicitous and cynical grandmother who herself struts about coolly but then obeys a
type of clumsy wisdom that's inside her head and keeps her
balanced.

March 3

François has left and Lori still hasn't talked to Maria. I'm
tempted to do it myself but I want her to face the situation,
it's up to her to make the omelet after she's broken the eggs.
I, who am the black sheep of the family, I, who take all those
liberties that everyone is ready to fault me for, in the eyes of
my granddaughter I look like the person who wants to restore
family order! It's totally laughable! I only want the truth. You
don't solve things by hiding the truth. On Maria's desk I saw
her notebooks all in order, the books by Flaubert and about
Flaubert, pen, pencils, erasers and the laptop she works on
when she's done with the notebooks. A nerd for a daughter?
A daughter most expert and knowledgeable in literary
matters but clueless when it comes to real life? Yet her
François stayed by her side, what does a small act of infidelity matter? But if that infidelity brings to life a child,
that's when it matters, and the future becomes complicated
and unpredictable. What will Maria do when she finds out
her most beloved François mated with her most beloved
Lori and that the two secretly conceived a child?

March 20

Yesterday I sat down next to mom who was cleaning string
beans to talk to her, I even started to tell her something but
she was distracted and I understood that it wasn't the right
moment, but will that moment ever arrive? the days go by,

François left for Lille and mom has started writing him long letters again, I watch her and I feel like a worm, but worms are blind and they eat without knowing what the future has in store for them, and if I am a larva instead, a larva that slides along and moves about awkwardly, knowing that it will soon transform into a butterfly and fly away? I don't know what to think, my thoughts freeze in my brain, cooled by doubts, what to do? what to decide? follow *nonna*'s advice or lie by saying the child is Tulù's and screw over my mother, François and Tulù? or, as I've always thought, resort to an abortion that would solve everything, no more baby, no more lies, deceits, truths to be revealed, all resolved with the snuffing out of a life?

March 30

I asked Lori if she told her mother, but she hasn't yet. Three months have already gone by and the idea of an abortion becomes more and more improbable. I'm afraid she'll choose the most cowardly path, that of attributing the child to Tulù, sparing both François and Maria. But what kind of sparing is that? A poor, distorted thing, that surely would be revealed maybe years later and then the consequences would be even more serious. One must never harbor lies that turn blood sour, and in any case, deceits are fed and result in rancor and a spirit of vengeance. In the meantime, poor Prometheus has died. We don't know what it may have eaten, maybe a poison that was spread on the ground by someone who wanted to kill some mice. Lori is inconsolable: she brought it to the public gardens and dug a hole to bury it, saying a prayer over its grave. Maria thinks she is inconsolable because the dog died, she can't guess the torment in her daughter's small sick brain, she has no clue of the baby that in the meantime is growing hair, forming the feet that will run along the road as soon as it comes out of that girl's belly. What will Maria do at the news of her beloved François's baby growing in her daughter's womb? Would she tell her to immediately go for an abortion or to keep it? Would she break it off with François or would she force him to marry her faithless daughter? I don't know or maybe I don't want to know: one knows nothing or at least very little of one's own children. So close to us and so far from our senses on alert. That's why some mothers and some fathers turn into spies and interrogators of their own children; not being able to control them, they want to possess them through a means of age-old authority and end up in the hell of a desire to dominate.

April 2

Prometheus is dead, the veterinarian had told me that if she didn't get better in a day or so she could die because the poison was making its way through that furry little body, all her cheerfulness suddenly left her, I would see her curled up under a chair or the kitchen table, her nose hot and dry, bleary-eyed, her rapid breathing, my poor little puppy who loved me so much, who came everywhere with me, even when I made love with François she was with me, and she looked at me as if she knew I was making a huge mistake, but she would never dream of scolding me like *nonna*, she would have simply smiled and told me to let this baby be born, because every birth is a joy, You could call it Prometheus like me, she would have said, for a fabled continuity between dogs and humans which you know is a matter of a deep and mysterious relationship in which everything seems improbable and instead becomes certain in the unbridled love which is established between the two, when I heard her gasp, I took her up in my arms and I saw her eyes that were staring at me asking for help, I started to cry, Don't go my darling little love, don't go, I beg you, what an unhappy fate you've had, poor Prometheus, first abandoned and then poisoned! I hugged her tight and I felt her slip away, she turned cold and stiff as I rocked her crying and singing to her the songs that mom would sing me to sleep when I was little, I brought her to the public gardens and I asked Goldie to help me bury her, and she was kind, she dug and dug without saying a word, then, before covering her with dirt, I gave her a maternal caress, in the end we sat near the grave drinking some coffee that I had brought with me in a thermos, Goldie gifted me one of her toothless disgusting but very tender smiles, she's the only person who doesn't judge me, she doesn't scold me even if after a while she gets bored and she turns her back on me to resume her iron work, Prometheus's death reinforced in me the idea of keeping the baby, I know now it's a boy, I saw it on the ultrasound, and even to tell my mom, truth has its reasons which reason does not know, I don't quite remember the phrase, or who said it, but it's sacrosanct, I want to face up to things, tell her everything but I don't know how, I just can't, I simply cannot.

April 10

Dear François,

It seems like yesterday we were strolling hand in hand through the flat streets of Amsterdam, we hunkered down in that little café near the elegant Tulip of Amsterdam hotel, do you remember? The glass door that quietly opened and closed, but each time it would let in a flurry of snow. Our fingers squeezed around a large cup of coffee to warm our hands, those lovely stuffed armchairs, those little apple pastries, they were delicious, we were away for two months and yet it felt like two days to me, now fixed and carved into my mind like a period of cheerful happiness. I have never loved you so much, and when you would wrap your arms around me in that huge bed covered with a duvet, puffy and so light, I felt like crying for joy. I do not think I have ever been so happy in my life.

Here at home, on the other hand, grumbling and discontent reign. All I hear are doors and windows slamming, my daughter is almost always out. Ever since Prometheus died, she has been ill-tempered, distant, and enraged. Do you remember how sweet and cheerful she was at Christmas, when you gave her the puppy and she seemed to love life, and you above all as you accompanied her to school every morning, you bought her new shoes, you gave her everything as if she knew she had found a new father. Now she barely looks at me. She passes by me in a huff and goes and locks herself in her room, or she silently waves to me as she goes out and I do not see her again until the evening.

Sometimes she comes home after we have already gone to bed. She tiptoes to the kitchen so as not to wake us up, drinks something and then again locks herself in her room. But I hear her all the same, I hear her bare feet on the tile floor, I hear the key in the lock and I ask myself why she is behaving this way. I have even persistently asked her what was wrong but she does not bother to answer. Oh man, mom, you don't understand anything, she answered, and went into the kitchen and then went out as usual slamming the door behind her. I asked my mother if she knew the reason for all this anger and silence but she said she knew nothing. As she uttered the word "nothing," however, she pursed her lips slightly as if she knew very well what was going on but she was forbidding herself from talking. She doesn't slam any doors, but she avoids me.

Apparently her baker friend has married. It is better that way, he is thirty years her junior, what good could possibly have come of it? Evidently she has started another game of love with a certain Filippo and they exchange a hundred thousand WhatsApp messages a day. Do you want to see how handsome he is? she asks, but I do not want to see him. I find that my mother exaggerates with all her small and superficial love affairs. How much younger is he than you? I asked her. Only fifteen years, she answered laughing. He has a wife and two daughters, only that his wife has her own life, they're practically separated under the same roof. And his daughters? They're teenagers and they don't care what their father does. It does not seem to be at all decent and with no prospect for the future. I would understand a late-age romance: it could happen, but with a married man who lives with his wife, it seems awkward to me, does his wife know? I asked her, but did not receive a reply. I imagine she does not know, poor woman, just think when she finds out that her husband is in love with another woman, with whom he exchanges steamy texts, as she confessed to me, even if they have actually never met. Technological devilry that I frankly find repulsive: a foreign object, a phantom object, that becomes concrete only on paper, actually on a video that never tells the truth, that proceeds by dint of lying words and photographs. Who knows how truthful the things he tells her really are: why in your opinion, would a forty-five-year-old, good-looking and well-off coffee salesman, according to what she tells me, why would such a man flirt with a sixty-year-old woman, as pleasing as she is, but almost twenty-years his senior, even if she confessed to be many years younger, but in the end we are talking about a stranger and she does not even know what he smells like, what his voice sounds like. It is a completely virtual love, it seems to me, that is inexistent, just the fruits of the captive fantasies of an electronic deceit.

But I will not bore you further with family matters. I want to give you some nice news: the tulips that I planted on the terrace have taken root and have sprouted some very green little leaves, pushing through the well-watered soil. It is such a pleasure to see those plants grow, a reminder of our happy adventurous days together. I can still see Van Gogh's paintings: his peasants bruised by hard labor but full of the joy of living, and then that world of stars that look like cauliflowers and skies furrowed with flocks of black birds that stand out against the yellow of the wheat. And way in the background, a small black figure that walks in the midst of the wheat field. It is the author, as the explanation suggests, or a pensive farmer who is on his way home, and then house and horizon are united in a single puffy and pearly line.

And do you remember when we ate at the self-service in the museum, when your tray fell with the plate, glass full of water and all? Fortunately they did not break but you turned red from embarrassment while I just laughed. The plate took off running vertically between the tables, and the glass jumped like a kangaroo: are they made of rubber? you asked, and we burst out laughing chasing the plate and glass that were escaping toward the door. And do you remember when we saw that man at the port who was buying raw herrings and tossed them whole into his mouth like a starving seal?

And the endless strolls along the canals? Once I was about to be hit by a bicycle, remember? I think we were walking on a bicycle lane where the cyclists race along without thinking twice, and when he miraculously avoided us, instead of stopping and asking our pardon, the cyclist began to yell at us. You had thrown yourself on me to save me from that maniac and we continued along holding on to each other. It is so important to detach from all the daily grind, from our too-close quarters and to go visit cities unknown, among never-before-seen faces trying to adapt to different ways of life.

Do you remember that early Monday morning when we found the door blocked by the bodies of two drunken young men who were sleeping so soundly that there was no way to move them, we ended up stepping over them, do you remember? As soon as we went out, we were embraced by a delicious warmth: the sun, after eight straight days of rain, snow and wind, came out hot, so sweet and unexpected. You took off your down jacket, but then not knowing what to do with it, put it back on. Who knows why every gesture of ours seemed awkward and funny, and made us laugh to tears. It is our honeymoon, you whispered in my ear. But we have been together for five years and taken many trips together! Well, a honeymoon as it should be, with lots of time at our disposal, we have never had that before, and this is just the thing. In fact, it was as if we had only gotten together a few days before. Your body had never adhered so well to mine since we have known each other. Your breath in mine, your tongue intertwined with mine, your eyes closed in the joy of sweet, profound, never-before-experienced sex.

I am very sorry it is over even if it lasted so long, we had never allowed ourselves such a long time together, you with your business and me with my translations, but this time we had to do it because we deserve much joy and much love, you said, and I no longer felt guilty for the translations I was neglecting.

With infinite love, my dear François,
I embrace you with all my heart.
Maria

April 15

Nonna says that if I don't talk to mom by the end of this week she's going to. No, *nonna*, please, can't you see how happy she is? She showed me all the pictures from their trip, a trip that he wanted to call *our honeymoon*, they're always stuck to each other and they love each other more than ever and I have to stick a knife in these two passionate hearts? How can I, tell me, how can I? I would gladly stick a knife in François's fickle heart, but not in mom's, that's bursting with love, just like one of those tulips that she brought back in her suitcase and that's about to blossom.

I get on my moped, go to the supermarket, fill a bag with stuff to eat and bring it to Goldie who thanks me with one of her sticky kisses, I told her I'm expecting a baby but I don't think she understood me, she lives in a world all her own, where words are useless and thoughts fly away like free and busy birds, I also brought her a duvet that I found at home, I think it's *nonna*'s, but she hasn't used it in years and it was just lying there gathering moths, Goldie are you happy? she doesn't answer, she doesn't speak, if she smiles at me with that toothless mouth it's already something, she snatches what I brought her from my hands and she teases me as snot drips from her nose, I offered to take her to a community center I know so that she could have a bed, but she shook her head with determination, she considers the garbage dump near the bridge her home, she built herself a roof of corrugated material—which I'm afraid is made of asbestos—and crooked walls by nailing together some wood from a chicken coop, at least I think they come from a chicken coop because stuck to the cracked and broken boards are small feathers of every color that every once in a while fall off and fly in the air, on the ground she's made herself a bed with an old filthy mattress that's certainly full of fleas, but she's fine there, she considers herself free and mistress, and even if she hasn't eaten for a few days because she hasn't found anyone who would give her some change, it's ok all the same, I discovered that she has some books near her bed. Goldie, you read? She nodded, And what do you read? she showed me the books, well-worn with soiled covers, pages missing, there's a book on cats, a book on the Greek Cynics, a copy of *The Little Prince*, of *Uncle Tom's Cabin*, she found them in the trash and she keeps them with care, I told her about my unwanted child and of the mess of a family that is hurting one another, she doesn't hear me anyway and is not listening to me, at one point she clapped her hands and laughed as if I were telling her the funniest thing in the world, Goldie, I'm telling you about a tragedy, but she just kept on clapping her hands, I still don't get how much she actually hears with those dirty ears of hers, I wondered how she manages to wash herself, but she must every so often, then I found out that when she has some money, she takes refuge in the bathroom at the station where there are even paid showers and she washes herself good and clean, even her long white hair, Goldie, you're a phenom, do you want more books? I'll bring you some, but she shakes her head, I don't know how deaf she is and to what extent she shuts off her ears when she doesn't want to hear, she could even be totally deaf and understands me because she reads lips, when she opens wide her liquid and lost eyes, I think she's not very different from one of those medieval mystics that my mom talks about, who would retreat to live in a cave, eating only herbs, but the mystics did it out of their love for Christ their spouse, Goldie does it for the love of freedom, which she may feel more like a spouse just like the mystics who thought of the wounded body of Christ as their husband, the mystic found peace in the beauty and solitude of a mountain, Goldie finds her peace in the trash of a city that is dirty, confused, and out of control, I brought her some instant coffee and she kissed my hand with great respect, But where will you get hot water? turning her back to me, she began to light a small fire, I have no idea where she found the matches, she's very skilled at lighting a tiny bonfire that is just enough to warm up a tin can full of river water.

Tulù and I are at it again big time, love seems to have returned hot and impetuous: can a pregnant woman arouse new desires? He doesn't know I'm expecting, but my body does, and it has ignited like a sun that emanates soft, hot rays, it must be so, because on the street men look at me as if they want to eat me up, luckily you still can't see much and I dress in baggy clothes that work well, but it won't be long before I won't be able to hide my belly and then all the knots will come to a head and I'll be forced to tell the truth; but what is truth anyway? a useless credulity in my opinion, when did truth ever lead to joy? only hurt, anger and retaliation, in my opinion truth is a stupid thing which should be hidden as best as possible, it just does damage and forces people to make stupid decisions, unfortunately, however, a child is more than a truth, it is a witness and I have to come up with something to make it acceptable, anyway I've decided to keep it, I'll keep it as best I can, and I'm not afraid of being a single teenage mom: if they help me out, fine, otherwise I'll make do, I'll do like that Peruvian girl who used to go clean in one of the publishing houses where mom worked: she would bring her newborn baby with her in a basket that she would place on the floor, never too far from where she was mopping, sweeping or vacuuming, and the baby, more precisely the little girl, her name was Estrellita, had already understood that she had to be still if she wanted to stay by her mother and in fact she stayed calm and still in her basket and when she was hungry she would call her mother by moving her little legs which she would wave in the air as if performing a ballet, her little bare feet would yell out instead of her voice which she had learned to hold back in her throat, and that's what I'll do if my mother throws me out, I could go to François, who at least with her showed himself to be protective and loving, but I'm afraid he won't welcome me with open arms: after his old mother's death he's living with a paralytic uncle, that's what he told me, I don't think there'll be enough room for me and the baby. I'll get a job and I'll bring the child along as the Japanese do, wrapped in a cloth and tied behind my shoulders with his knees on each side of my hips, finding food for him and for me, my mom, she would have every reason to throw me out, I really screwed up this time, as long as she doesn't make too much of a fuss, I hate to see her cry, even if it's actually been years since she's cried, ever since dad passed, thin as a rail, after all the treatments they put him through, even a transplant, he seemed cured of the disease and instead it came back with a vengeance and it ate him up in the blink of an eye, he was pale and his face was as swollen as a soccer ball, his hair had fallen out, he looked a hundred years old even though he wasn't quite forty, I was so angry as a child that he had gone without even saying goodbye, but when I look at the photograph where he and I are walking along a narrow country road, followed by a black-and-white dog, I feel that I loved him very much and maybe something of that love is buried somewhere: I can see him racing along on his bike, as he used to do when I was little, carrying me on the back seat, Hang on tight otherwise you'll fall, he would say to me, and once we actually did fall, but we didn't get hurt, we held on to each other as we rolled around in the grass.

May 2

Filippo has become obsessive: he wants to know what I'm doing every minute, where I'm going, whom I'm seeing, as if he were my boyfriend. We've never even seen each other, Filippo, what claims do you have on me? He says he loves me by the strength of a feeling that he hadn't anticipated and that it's jeopardizing his family to whom he is bound as by a fate that holds him captive. Filippo, we don't know each other, I have no idea what you're like, let's leave things as they are, this long-distance love warms my heart, why do you want to force things?

He answers by saying that he has seen me a thousand times through pictures: don't we send each other pics through WhatsApp, don't we have an idea of what we look like? Yes, but pictures lie Filippo, I, for example, have lied to you, I'm not forty years old but sixty and I'm a grandmother to a grand-daughter who's about to make me a great-grandmother. I had to tell him because he was tormenting me almost as if I were his property acquired by computer love. I didn't read or hear from him for five days; WhatsApp, with his photo in the magic miniature circle, didn't vibrate to grab my attention.

On the sixth day I heard the beep and there he was again. Your age doesn't matter, Gesuina, I love you for what you write, for your mind, for the body I see in your pictures, tell me at least that the pictures are real and are yours, tell me that you're not some hunchbacked wrinkled old lady but a lovely woman, tall and shapely as I see in the photographs. The photos are from this year and some from last year, I'm just as you see me, Filippo. That satisfied him and he sent me so many smiling emojis. Nevertheless, I think it's extraordinary that a forty-five-year-old man has fallen in love, even if through images, with a sixty-year-old woman, and he feels the need to write to me and check up on me.

In my opinion, even he doesn't want to meet, but to possess me through the ether, to virtually make me his, all his and ready for an embrace that will never happen even if it will happen all the time in his imagination and perhaps even in mine. The only thing is I don't feel this need to possess: I know he has a wife, two daughters with whom he is very close and I would never expect him to leave them to come and live with me. I wonder if we women have unconsciously incorporated a sense of propriety on ourselves, I don't mean social, but deeper, regarding modesty and habits of feeling, which men on the other hand have not, used as they are to appropriating women's bodies as they please. Bodies that when they grow distant and show reluctance and independence arouse their anger, jealousy, their resolve to possess and dominate. But this is more like an argument that my daughter, Maria, would make, not so customary to my lips, out of character for me and my mental habits. Am I turning into her? are my pressing years softening and fading me? is Lori's pregnancy making me change my style?

I've never told Filippo about Simone the baker, but if he were to find out, what would he do? Probably nothing, because even that story would fall in the area of virtuality and would transform into angry and insulting words. And if instead, as seems to happen every day, Filippo were to arm himself with a knife and come to kill me and Simone? Besides, what is the relationship between imagination and reality? I must ask my daughter, Maria, who is the scholar in the family and reads all manner of books, even ones on psychology in addition to history and philosophy. But Maria is lost in her amorous delusions. She can't even imagine the tremendous blow that is about to land on her head. And it will be her own daughter who will give it to her, the blow that will knock her out. Poor Maria! Yet, it's good that she knows how things are, we can't go on living in the clouds and in the fiction that chains us in this house together. I'd like to keep out of it but I'm up to my neck in it despite my love affairs. Everything is complicated Gesuina, everything, there is nothing truly clear and as to be expected. We're caught in a dark cloud hoping it will dissipate but in the meantime we can't even see where our feet land.

May 10

Dear François,

There is a secret going around in this house that belongs to my mother and my daughter. I caught some strange looks between them: what is going on? It is as if they were hiding something from me, but what? In a small female community, everything goes round, nothing escapes notice, above all the possession of a secret that passes from one brain to another, revealing itself through quick mysterious glances, but in this case involves only two minds, the third being left aside unaware and ignored. I do not even understand whether the secret is about me in some way. But if they are so determined to hide it from me, I cannot help but think that it is about me. Is it about me, Lori? I would like to ask her because she seems to be the most upset by this secret, but she keeps her lips sealed and does not answer my queries.

Forgive me if I bore you with my family tales. Sometimes I ask myself why I am always the one to talk to you about my homelife and my family while you remain quiet about your homelife and your family, small as it is, if, as you tell me, you've been living in Lille with a paralytic uncle since your mother's death. Contrary to my mother, who keeps up a correspondence with a certain Filippo on WhatsApp and knows everything about him and shows me his pictures, I have never seen your house, I have never seen a picture of your mother, I do not know what the room you sleep in looks like, the kitchen where you have your coffee in the morning, the face and body of this paralytic uncle about whom you have only recently hinted to me. Does the fact that we are both resistant to technology make us more distant from and ignorant of each other? But on the other hand, you often tell me: love is the only truth between us, the rest does not matter. And in fact when we are together we are like two lovers at their first meeting: peers, free, happy to be together, to embrace, to laugh, to kiss, it is all so easy and perfect. Though sometimes I feel as though we were suspended in a light, iridescent bubble, a bubble that could explode at any moment precisely because the fate of bubbles is to disappear after having dissolved into a thousand pieces. Perhaps I am exaggerating. There is something far more concrete and stable between us; there is an understanding between two adult and consenting bodies that seek each other out, find each other, mate, and take pleasure in doing so. Let us not forget this decisive detail: we are not just two dreamers in love with love, but two people who know each other better and better, who write each other sincerely, even our most remote thoughts, and as soon as they can, plan beautiful vacations together, and when they meet, they embrace with an ever-renewing joy. It is not trivial, François, perhaps it is a great deal, so much, the whole reality of the universe is enclosed in this small world of thoughts and facts that weighs as much as a whole ox, in the moment we are together we are one person, or perhaps two in one, I cannot tell, but I feel you are a part of me and the rest does not matter as you say.

Last night I dreamed of you again. I held you close to me as always, but then suddenly I realized I was holding tight a strange being with slippery and slimy skin. I shivered with fear, in fact I realized I was holding in my arms an enormous crocodile with hard, thick scales. I let out a scream and woke up. How I managed to have such a foolish dream, I do not know. . . . The crocodile did not want to hurt me, though; it just embraced me. Do you realize the oddity of it? A crocodile on me, with its wet paws that clung to my sides and its long, bristling mouth with a double row of teeth wanted to kiss mine. How in the world can a crocodile mouth kiss a human mouth? When I woke up, I sensed the taste of salt water and seaweed. One's imagination can play such cruel tricks.

I embrace you with much love. See you soon,

Maria

May 21

Dear mom, actually dearest mom,

I decided to write you a letter because I can't manage to say it out loud. . . . I want to first state that my love for

you is crazy, as deep as a well and from that well I've
always drawn good water to drink, a light, sweet clean,
fresh water like no other water, mom, so here I am about
to confess to you that in the well, I, with the irresponsibil-
ity of an egotistical child, have thrown, almost unwill-
ingly, but with a mean gesture, something that has
poisoned the waters, we have to close that well, mom,
because it could send us to the netherworld. You will say
to me: what are you talking about, Lori? What is this play
on words? What do you want to say to me? And I will
answer that I can't manage to tell you because I know
I would stick a knife in your chest, but at the same time,
as *nonna* believes, I have to tell you because any truth,
even hard, bitter, murderous truth, is better than a lie, the
truth I have to tell you is about François, I know how
much you love each other, I know you are two bodies that
have met, chosen and know each other and love each other
but love falls asleep sometimes, even for a few seconds,
François and I made love, but I swear to you without any
feelings, and from that moment of foolishness a baby was
conceived, there, that's the secret that I've been holding on
to for months and is making me die of anguish, I should
have confessed it to you before, *nonna* has been telling me
so from the moment she found out and maybe she's right,
she forced me to tell you, it's important, and you have to
know that I don't love François, and he doesn't love me,
I behaved despicably and like a fool, but now the omelet
is done, as *nonna* says, and if you'll want to kick me out,
I'll understand, I'll make do, with the baby and without
a man by my side, don't blame François because he truly
loves you and he considers this small vile act closed, he
doesn't know about the baby, and if you want, we won't
even tell him, we'll keep the secret to ourselves and we'll

raise this baby just the three of us, you *nonna* and me, even
if I don't dare hope for such a dream, that would be too
good to be true, I know that it would be a tragedy for you:
you would have to leave François who loves you and whom
you love and I don't want to ruin this great love, even if
I contributed to its ruin, maybe I was envious of your
beautiful union, maybe I was hoping to make him mine
by secretly stealing him, but I really think that in the end
I will go away, for the moment I'll ask my friend Agatha
to put me up, just the other day she told me she left her
husband and would like to have someone in the house to
keep her company, not only would she have my company
but the company of the newborn as well, who I hope will
be as quiet as Estrellita, the daughter of the Peruvian
woman who used to clean the publishing house where you
worked, do you remember her? you told me her story, the
young mother—what was her name? I don't remember—
who would bring her newborn Estrellita to work in a
basket and she would move her to wherever she happened
to be cleaning, either when she was mopping the floor, or
when she would make coffee for the office workers, and
since the baby was very quiet, no one had anything to
complain about, I'll do the same, mom, I'll make do, don't
worry, there, I must confess that I feel so relieved of the
weight of this great secret that I feel like flying, I've
become light, oh so light, ready to take flight, I'd love to
perch myself on the ceiling while you read this letter so
that I can see how you'll react, don't hate me too much,
mom, my love for you has not changed, I could've had an
abortion, but from the time I felt this baby move inside
me, the idea of throwing him out became more and more
difficult for me, I had thought of saying it was Tulù's child
and I spoke to *nonna* about it but she rightly said that in

that way not only would I jerk around me you and François, but even Tulù, not to mention that the child would have grown up with a father who wasn't his, too many knots to unravel and I'm very good at creating them, sailor's knots, fisherman's knots, double, triple locking knots, but I'm horrible at unraveling them, mom, I've told you everything, now I'll wait for you to say the word, whatever your decision I'll accept it without protest, I'm wrong and you're right, even if I know that being right in this case will give no sense of satisfaction but only worries and hurt, don't blame François, it's all my fault.

I embrace you with all my heart, your
Lori

May 22

This morning Lori came to wake me screaming. She pulled me by the arm toward Maria's bedroom. She was lying neatly on her bed, all dressed, except for her sweaty forehead and hair plastered to her skull. I don't know how many sleeping pills she took. My hands were shaking when I tried to take her pulse, which was still there but weak and sluggish, almost nonexistent. I called for an ambulance while Lori wandered around the house not knowing what to do. As I quickly dressed I heard her sobbing. Instead of crying, get dressed and come with me to the emergency room! But I understood that she just could not. So I took off as soon as the ambulance came and I went to the hospital with Maria.

I watched as the two EMTs tied her to the cot with the engine roaring and straining to push its way through traffic. Once we arrived, I wanted to go into the operating room with her and the nurses but they didn't let me. Sit here and wait, we'll tell you when you can go in. And they disappeared. I heard them pumping her stomach. Horrible sounds of vomiting, of desperate coughing, of voices that hurriedly alternated. After an hour they came out with the stretcher. She was on it, pale as death but still alive, I saw her dull eyes, her drawn face, her swollen neck. Thank you for saving her! But the stretcher was racing and the male nurses were pushing it along very long hallways. I ran with them. Where are you taking her? We have to intubate her and set her up in the room. Which room? In the intensive care unit. But why? You can't come in, you can't come in.

Now the nurse was one, and he had bare, tattooed arms. I tried to say something to my daughter, but my words did not reach her. The hallways gave way to other hallways. I followed those tattoos, fascinated with their ugliness. A mermaid with her long-haired head peering out on the nurse's shoulder, and a long fish tail that ran along his right arm. On his other arm, a ship with all its sails unfurled. At every movement of his muscles, the sails seemed to fill with wind and proceed toward the horizon. At the same time, the mermaid wagged her tail. The mermaid and boat will never meet outside of those muscular arms and yet they swell and move as if they were alive.

May 30

I'm next to my daughter's bed, in a room with another three comatose women. They had me slip on a green lab coat, with a cap on my head, my hands disinfected, my shoes wrapped in two plastic bags that make me walk as if I were on clouds. Maria's been in a coma for days. She's breathing. Her heart is beating, her eyelids are closed. Her locked lips open only to allow a tube to pass through that nourishes her artificially.

My eyes mechanically follow the arms of the male nurse who moves about the beds of the sick.

Does the black-inked mermaid want to board the ship? Perhaps to fall in love with one of the sailors who hoist the sails by the mere strength of their arms and climb up the great mast in the center of the boat to scan the horizon? But would a sailor even fall in love with a mermaid? Legend says it's the mermaid who falls in love with a sailor. Mermaids, however, as the legend goes, bring bad luck and one must steer clear of their bewitched bodies. Nevertheless, the half-fish woman keeps following the ship and the more the sailors become aware of her presence, the more the sea swells, the wind rages and places everyone's life at risk.

At that point the captain realizes that the mermaid is in love with one of his sailors and he decides to draw lots for the name of one of them to throw overboard to calm the waters. A young and handsome sailor turns out to be the one chosen by chance. But that young man is also his best, and the captain decides to give him a second and even a third chance, but each time he draws lots, his name comes out: he must be the very one the mermaid loves, and so, albeit reluctantly, the captain decides to throw him overboard, but the sailor stops him saying: You're right, my name came out three times, therefore it is I who must be sacrificed to save the ship, but before throwing me overboard, leave me alone with the mermaid. They leave him alone and he leans aft, where the mermaid appears and disappears, and he sings her a beautiful, sad and languid Irish song, but so sweet that the mermaid, cradled by that voice and that beautiful melody, is placated and the sea immediately becomes calm and the ship can continue on its journey without sacrificing the handsome sailor.

The boat that tosses about on his bare arms and the mermaid that swims in the turbulent waters and listens to the suave voice of the sailor accompany the pain that I am unable to put to rest. The sailor is not there. There aren't any human bodies in the images sketched on skin. Who knows when and where I read this tale that comes to mind in this moment as I observe the nurse's tattoos. As much as I force myself to focus my eyes on Maria, scanning her motionless face, I can't help but observe spellbound those arms that move securely and efficiently, but at the same time dismembered and terrible with the coldness of fate.

It hurts too much to stare at my daughter's ashen and motionless face for long. Please, mom, don't die, says Lori, who's seated in the hallway and with whom I take turns next to Maria's bed. Even François has come and is sitting at the edge of his seat, quiet and pale, looking at his hands. He doesn't speak, doesn't eat, he looks broken. But he created this trouble, actually she did, they both did. They look desperate, Lori and he, and they keep their distance from each other, now that he knows what happened and her belly is showing, he doesn't even grace her with a look, but you can tell that her closeness worries him.

June 4

My belly's growing and school's almost over, finally, even though I haven't gone to school very much recently, the baby paws at me, I wanted François to feel its kicks by placing his hand on my stretched-out skin, but he didn't want to, he formed two deep wrinkles on his forehead which he didn't have before this suicide, that's what he said, as if mom were dead, But she's alive, I insisted, she's in a coma and we don't know when she'll come out of it, maybe in a few days, or a few years, so says the doctor who looks at me as if I were a dumb tramp, like Goldie, my hair's a mess, my belly lifts up my skirt, a sweater that's too loose and slips on my hips, and the air of someone who can't breathe well and has too many pine cones in her head, I can't look at her lying on the bed like that, my mother, closed in the intensive care unit, among those people, who is barely breathing, doesn't see, doesn't speak, was I wrong to write that letter? I'd like to ask François but he's not speaking and not listening, I'd like to ask *nonna* but even she seems to be deaf, as if it were entirely my fault, Mom, please don't die, we need you and besides I don't want to live my life feeling sorry about telling you the truth, please, mom, open your eyes, look at me, tell me that you're still here, I'm lost without you, I knew that the truth is something foolish and dangerous, a poison that can kill, I told *nonna* so, yet she insisted and even my son Prometheus told me, with his language of kicks in my belly, that I had to tell the truth, at the cost of messing things up, but life is a mess, mom, it's not my fault or François's, but tell me how I can fix this, tell me, please, and I'll do it, the baby seems calm and happy, he continues to grow peacefully, sending me now and then a volley of kicks that makes me feel nauseated, the gynecologist Amelia says he's big and healthy and that he'll be born in September and he will do great things because he has the strength of a young bull and the impetus of a kid goat who butts even before he comes out, You should have foreseen the consequences, *nonna* shouts at me, But how, when, how? one doesn't think of the consequences, Because you, Lori, are not responsible, she says, a responsible person is one who foresees the consequences of her actions, that's what it means to be responsible, You've already said so, many times, *nonna*, but it doesn't seem to me that you are so much more responsible than me, with all your old lady love affairs, I know what I'm doing and I don't cheat anyone, she yells, I don't steal, I don't deceive, I don't mess up, my love affairs are out in the open, but I know very well that's not true because she has deceived more than Mata Hari herself.

June 7

François has left. Mournful, quiet, pale. It's not your fault, François, our bodies sometimes betray us, normally there are no consequences but in this case you two conceived a child and everything became more complicated. Will he be as handsome as you, this baby that Lori wants to call Prometheus, seems like bullshit to me. It didn't bring any luck to the puppy and in historical memory it's linked to a treacherous fate: a man chained to a rock, whose liver is continually pierced and devoured by the voracious beak of an eagle. A ferocious punishment for a sin I don't get: for having stolen fire from the gods to give it to mankind, after all wasn't it a wonderful conquest for us? Why punish him so cruelly? But now that I think of it, I understand that, for the person in command in those heavens inhabited by vengeful tyrants, it is an unforgivable sin. Was Prometheus merely a Titan who entered into disgrace with the heavenly powers that be? Or was he a friend of progress who so infuriated those persons who wanted man to remain submissive and obedient? I don't know, but François, who knows myths well, says that he was a hero. Whereas Lori doesn't know anything about it and places her trust in an oral memory that reminds her of her mother and her puppy who died prematurely.

June 15

Hello, hello, it's me, my little tape recorder, today you turned on sooner than expected . . . but does it make any sense to talk into a machine? And who should I talk to then? Only you listen to me and seal my words with serene fastidious-ness. That's why it's worth trusting in you, my precious little machine.

I want to begin with little Prometheus who is kicking inside his mother's belly, while she gorges herself on ice cream that soothes her inflamed throat. You should call him Little Strawberry, I say, because she adores strawberry ice cream. Meanwhile Maria is still in a coma in the intensive care unit, and laziness is winning over diligence, we go less often to visit her in the hospital. It's as if my sorrowful daughter wishes to die without dying: she's there mute and unmoving, with her eyes closed, in a huge room with many other beings with immobile bodies, in the silence of a room in which only the oxygen tubes hiss. François calls often to find out how his Maria is doing, but he doesn't ever ask about the baby. He ignores it and Lori feels bad, even if she continually declares that the child is hers and no one else's and she will raise him by herself without needing anyone. A slightly insolent and presumptuous statement. In the meantime, she doesn't do shit and I'm the one who has to run the household: groceries, cooking, washing clothes, straightening up, sweeping the floor: my back is a mess.

The work of an unlicensed nurse with skilled hands has doubled, luckily. Now I go out at all hours to give shots for a fee. You can't imagine how many people need shots: for the flu, for liver disease, for diabetes, for rhinitis, for a stomachache, for asthma and you can't imagine how scared they are of a syringe as they timidly uncover their behinds with fear of that needle, especially children and the elderly, but I reassure them and when they realize that they didn't even feel the pinch, they call me back for every silly indisposition.

Lori asks me what asses I notarized today but I no longer have the desire or the energy to dwell on the language of asses. I uncover them, I prick them, and then off I run. You no longer read the constellation of moles on your clients' backs? No, Lori, I'm too tired and always in a hurry, I don't have time. And I ask myself, are we really becoming accustomed to this shitty life? Maria in the hospital in intensive care, me going around poking holes in butts and Lori who's getting bigger and bigger and heavier and doesn't want to move except to go to the ice-cream parlor to buy herself a cone. She fills up with ice cream, especially strawberry. The child will be born with a strawberry birthmark on his butt, I tell her to try to get her to walk more, to stop stuffing herself, but she doesn't listen to me. She just lies there sprawled out on the couch watching these shows with guns that shoot and belts that strangulate and knives that slit throats: I have no idea what perverse mind creates them.

Her mother, if she would see her like that, would urge her to read. Read, my dear Lori, because books make your mind blossom, they put down deep roots which then fill with sap and produce airy and perfumed flowers, your head is stuffy, give it some air, read! But she, who drags her big belly around as if it were a weight that does not concern her, has become apathetic and very lazy. From her bed she moves to the couch, and from the couch to her bed. She doesn't even think of calling François who's waiting for word of his beloved: she doesn't read, she doesn't speak, I don't even know whether she pays attention to those foolish stories that scroll across the screen. She just lies there motionless, almost imitating her mother, who can't move and is fed through all sorts of tubes. And what about Tulù? I ask her worriedly. She answers with a shrug. Did you break up with him? He's the one who broke up with me when he learned of the baby that's not his. Is that why you're in such a foul mood? Who told you I'm in a foul mood, *nonna*? You don't understand anything. But she says it with such anger and such malice that it only confirms my idea that she is in a very foul mood.

July 3

Here I am again, speaking to you, stupid shitty machine. Maria lies unhearing and unspeaking; Lori attacks me every time I say something to her. The hospital called. A very kind doctor told me they need Maria's bed, that they will help us in every way but we have to take her home. So that means she's better? I commented nearly crying from joy. She's stationary, was the reply, and we don't really know how long it will last, that's why you must bring her home. In that condition, in a coma, and who will take care of her? The hospital will help you set up a room, a nurse will come to see her every day according to the international protocol for people who are in a vegetative state; you'll provide her with artificial nutrition through the tracheostomy tube, you have the right to a "service card" that will provide you home-nursing assistance, we'll furnish the oxygen and all the necessary equipment, all will go well, you'll see. Enough with all the medical jargon that is intended to not let anything be understood by the sick person and the caregiver.

How will we manage to take care of her? I asked anxiously. You'll learn, the doctor pronounced, looking me in the eyes with an ironic and at the same time punitive air. Dr. Salsa's not all that good-looking, Lori says, he doesn't have a chin and his mouth is attached directly to his neck. And yet he has something attractive about him: two big, sparkling eyes, two long arms with gigantic hands attached with clean well-trimmed fingernails. With those hands he could hold up the world, like Atlas, and place it on his shoulders to take it home. A world heavy with the sick and people in a coma for years. But how long could it last, doctor, is there a possibility that Maria will come back to life? Yes, there are possibilities, but we don't know how many. You see, once, it was easy to understand if a person was dead or alive, today things are complicated; there was a time when there weren't any machines that kept the central pump, that is the heart, in action, even if the brain had stopped working, dear Gesuina, there weren't any oxygenators or feeding tubes that would have kept with us people who in other times would have been considered lost. That's why it's difficult to decide whether to insist on care, that some call *therapeutic persistence*, or let them go by removing the feeding tube and artificial respiration. What would you do, doctor? I don't know, I think you have to wait and then you'll decide. But how long? A few months, a year? And if she doesn't give any signs of life? I can't say: if you think it's time to pull the plug, you will, otherwise you'll continue to keep her on artificial life support. You certainly are a big help, Dr. Salsa. And he takes my hand in his, he squeezes it and smiling he says: You need a lot of patience, Gesuina, and I know you have it. Take care of your daughter with love, sometimes love makes miracles. Sometimes, I know, but not always, I answer back. He laughs and walks away sliding away in the clogs of a doctor on call.

July 10

Mom's back home, stretched out and motionless, her snow-white hands resting on her chest, as if she were dead, but she's not dead, fortunately, and now she'll be here with us, while Prometheus grows, she sleeps, might there be a happy prince who will come to wake her up? All it takes is a kiss, says *nonna*, but François is in his Lille and he phones more and more rarely, every once in a while he calls but he doesn't talk much, he asks about Maria and sighs when we tell him she's still in a coma, he hangs up without adding anything else, I believe he's getting used to the idea of losing her, occasionally I talk to him about the baby, but he cuts me off as if the child weren't his. He's your son! I want to shout at him, but I don't because you can't force a child on someone, if he wants him, he'll seek him out, this arrogance of his gets on my nerves, as if the baby is at fault, as if he were there by accident, even if it is in fact the case, more than love, sexual attraction, this baby is born by accident, little Prometheus pops out by accident, and yet he willfully wanted to be born, steal fire from death and grasp onto life, that's why I want to call him Prometheus, I will defend him against everything and everyone, a mother and son are the most powerful force in the world, they can challenge the universe, by dint of bites and hugs they will always manage because the future depends on these two united bodies that feed on each other, who go hand in hand toward the shitty future that we know all too well, but they will go and will never lose their way because the next few hours, the next few years are all for them.

July 22

Life has become complicated, I had to learn the secret of the tubes: small ones, big ones, plastic ones, oil cloth, nylon, rubber, there are all kinds of them and you must be careful that they let flow the liquids that a woman in a vegetative state, like poor Maria, needs. Attached to each tube is a little metal valve that regulates the flow of the fluid. The nurse taught me how to insert the tube into the small faucet that Maria has inserted into her chest, under her left shoulder. Of course, each time the tubes need to be flushed and disinfected. Then there are the lighter tubes that are connected to a large bottle suspended on a gallows-shaped iron pole and that serves to feed her and pass through another little faucet tied to her pulse, and finally there's the catheter tube that empties out her urine into a bag hung on a hook attached to the bed. In short, Maria's body is an itinerary of pipes and tubes that chase each other, intertwine and overlap. A tangle of liquid streets, sweet little Maria, that crosses your motionless body, keeps you alive, but your brain, your brain that looks, understands, judges and decides, where is your brain? It's as if that walnut of intelligent and shocked swirls in your head were frozen and doesn't feel the warmth of the world that beats out the cold of inexistence, as if your body had returned millennia, to the Ice Age. But humans, our ancestors, on those occasions always moved south and the great migrations began. And you, Maria, when do you intend to begin your voyage toward the south, toward life, toward the sun-warmed world, toward us who are waiting for you as the alive and fruitful palms of the Africa of feelings? A somewhat literary prayer, I realize, my daughter, but it is precisely by resorting to the language that is familiar to you that I try to speak to you. If I were to address you with Lori's ramshackle and verbose words, not only would you not understand, but you would feel almost offended by the lack of air in the sentences.

The nurse with the tattooed arms, the one we met at the hospital, comes by almost every day. His name is Angelo, and he alternates with a woman called Alessia and she goes around with bare arms but has no signs of tattoos, but she wears glittering bracelets with little bells that dangle and ring with every movement of her pulse. Angelo is very good, he has delicate and quick hands, except that he's brusque, at times too fast and in fact he's had a few disasters, but then he quickly fixes it with his expert hands, and it seems to me Maria breathes more regularly when he is in the vicinity. On the other hand, Alessia is a slowpoke: she does everything extremely slowly and sometimes she forgets along the way what she was preparing and starts all over again. She taught me how to administer shots into the veins. It doesn't take much, you must tighten the tourniquet above the elbow and then feel for the vein that is most prominent, then tap lightly on top of it with your fingertips, and finally insert the needle almost horizontally and if you prick the vein right away, you're very good, otherwise you're a wreck. She always pierces it, but she told me there are some veins that run away like eels as soon as they sense the needle coming and it becomes very difficult to follow and catch them. You mean veins move? Yes, of course they move, like everything in the universe, she answered angelically, do you believe we remain still on this earth? Of course not, the world turns around at breakneck speed in the solar system and never stops, just like our cells never stop, they are born, reproduce and die every second. I look at her in admiration: for her the universe and the human body have no secrets, and she treats both with the same cordial, swift competence. We've become friends by now: as soon as Angelo arrives, he asks for a coffee and while he waits for it, he confidently enters into Maria's room, goes near the bed and with brusque gestures he turns her on her stomach uncovering her back to see if it has any signs of new wounds, if he finds any, he takes care of them with a cotton ball soaked in a pink disinfectant and a whitish cream that leaves his big hands greasy. He had me buy a sheepskin which, he claims, holds up better to the rubbing against her now muscleless skin. Then he checks the tubes, the valve and the faucet where the liquids enter. After that he takes her temperature, blood pressure, notes everything down on a piece of paper and runs off after hastily downing his hot coffee. While he's working, I observe him. The mermaid and ship are still there to reassure my restless gaze. I wonder if the mermaid in love with the mysterious sailor will ever reach her beloved man or if she will be forced for her whole life to chase after that ship with great unfurled wings racing toward the future, imprisoning in its bosom the beautiful and unreachable body of the young navigator.

Maria's care has distracted me from the real and fake loves that I was used to, it has distanced me from the games that warmed my days. Life has given me a blow to the head just as it did to Maria, it has placed two shackles on my ankles and now I must spend more and more time at home, rush through the injections, and work mind, body, and soul if I want to keep this one-foot-in-the-grave daughter alive. I've almost forgotten the baker, even if the kisser always waits for me in his shop and as soon as he sees me, he calls me from afar and shows me the bread he's set aside for me. I have to admit, his loyalty to kisses is touching. This is for you, I don't want anything, but come in for a moment, and he pulls me toward the back of the shop, where we can kiss, even if in a rush. The kiss, Gesuina, is the salt of life, he whispers in my ear and presses his soft and gentle lips, which have a sweet smell of leavened bread, on my lobe. I must admit that, despite my impatience, his kisses have preserved something of the old emotions. Simone knows how to kiss boldly and shyly with sweetness and energy. His kisses, as he theorizes, are predictable and poignant at the same time. I always come out of it a little shaken. I'm in a hurry, Simone, let me go, my daughter's home alone and I have to take care of her. This loaf is for your bedridden daughter, he says, even if he knows very well that Maria doesn't eat, doesn't talk, doesn't shit, doesn't see, barely breathes. I've explained it to him, but each time Simone pretends he's forgotten and hands me the bread whispering: For the lovely Maria! And with the bread tucked under my arm, off I hurry toward home where Lori ever remains, since she almost never goes out now, though I can't trust her to take care of anything.

Filippo's lost in the ether of the web. He must have found another woman to love and control remotely. We never met even if his posts had lately become almost insulting for their constant suspicions and constant injunctions. Where were you? With whom? What did you do? Did you think of me? How often? Why didn't you answer my WhatsApp at 12:10? Filippo, I have things to do, I'm not a housewife, that too, yes, maybe, but besides the house I have to think about the injections I have to give around the neighborhood to earn a living. Who do you give shots to, only women or men too? Well, Filippo, I can't discriminate, I go wherever they send me, I give shots to both women and men. Very bad, you shouldn't uncover men's butts, you're a degenerate and so on. He expected to possess me from a distance and control me as if I were his property. When I told him about my comatose daughter, though, I felt him retreat like a snail into its shell. He wrote for a few more days but vaguely, making strange excuses, and then he disappeared. All this love melted away like snow in the sun and not long after he stopped writing entirely. It's better that way. I really don't have time now to play at love.

When Maria was alive and active, I considered myself more a daughter than a mother; now I have to be the mother to a daughter who is no longer my mother but hopelessly my daughter and dependent on me for every need of her inert body. The sleeping beauty, as Lori calls her, who awaits the kiss of her handsome prince. But will this handsome prince ever come? When? Where? And will he stay should he decide after all to come? And if he shouldn't come at all? Damn waiting, which keeps us in suspense and always on the alert. We eagerly await a smile, a whispered word, a bat of a lash, small and revolutionary gestures that now seem increasingly improbable to us, and yet we are certain that they may surprise us and as a result they keep us alert throughout the day and into the night.

I don't sleep very much now, actually very little; whereas before I would sleep my eight hours, now I probably sleep more or less three or four hours, always with an ear to Maria's breathing, always ready for a call, for a word from her. And between one awakening and the other, I have heavy, disturbing dreams. The other night I dreamed of a two-headed dog that stood before me and with a very human voice it spoke to me of Prometheus and it told me that I had to organize an expedition to the highest mountains to free him from the voracious eagle. Doesn't that Frenchman of yours also reiterate that Prometheus is a hero? So why do you leave him up there to suffer tied to that rock? I thought: yes, it's right, but where is this rock, and how do I get there? The dog was not listening to me; it was shaking in a rather disturbing way its two big heads with thick hair that formed a crown around its snout. Maybe it's a lion with two heads? A creature from the darkest and most disturbing forests? I didn't see its teeth while it was talking, but I did see its black lips and its eyes staring at me sternly.

6:00 P.M.

I'm a bit worried because Lori had some strong belly pains and I feared she would have a miscarriage. I called Dr. Amelia asking if she could please come to the house to examine her because Lori can't move and I can't bring her in and leave my comatose daughter alone. The doctor came; she examined her. She said the baby is growing, it's healthy, and perhaps too big and heavy for a mother not particularly muscular. She too insisted that Lori eat meat, fish and vegetables and not just ice cream, that she force herself to go for walks, because muscles are important and without muscles a child cannot manage to come out on its own, a cesarean section might be necessary, even if a natural birth is always preferable. It works for the first child, but for the second it becomes more difficult and that poor belly will transform into a sieve. Lori heard her out but shrugged. I don't think she feels like going out more than she does now.

Out of desperation, I called Tulù. Even if I don't know him, I know everything about him, and I'd like to speak to him about Lori. Tulù was kind but stern: Lori had a baby with someone else, let the father worry about it, I have nothing to do with it, besides, *signora*, let me tell you that I'm living with my new German girlfriend, her name is Andrea and we're in love. So there, stick that in your pipe and smoke it. I had to announce to Lori that Tulù had found a new love, her name is Andrea, she's German, she's a gym teacher and lives with him. Someone older than him, let him enjoy her! she commented, seemingly disinterested, but she appeared quite alarmed.

July 25

The other day as I entered the house I found the two nurses, Alessia and Angelo, having sex standing up next to Maria's bed. They were startled since they hadn't heard the door which I always open gently so as not to disturb the sleeping beauty. I discovered that when the doors slam, she gives a slight jolt. That means she hears noises. So there is something alive in her after all, I tell myself, and I'm caught up in such joy that all my tiredness dissipates.

Alessia, red faced, straightened her skirt and Angelo pulled up his pants with quick and blustery gestures, as if I were the guilty one to have bothered them in a licit and normal act: what of it, can't two young nurses have sex when and where they like? I didn't say a word of reproach; in fact I smiled commenting that love is life and maybe it can help a half-dead woman return among us. It was almost as if I were thanking them for what they were doing and they looked at me stunned. Where's Lori? I was amazed not to find her camped out on the couch. She went out, they answered, as if it were something normal. Went out where? and when is she coming back, did she say? But they knew nothing. And so yet another worry was born. Where must she have gone? She never leaves the house. Has she for once followed Dr. Amelia's orders? or did she throw herself in the river out of the desperation that has taken hold of her these days? I didn't call the police. What would I even say? My pregnant granddaughter left the house and I don't know where she went? They'd send me to hell. I'll wait a little longer.

8:00 P.M.

Lori did in fact come home. I screamed at her: Where have you been? You had me worried. Wherever the hell I wanted, she answered arrogant and angry. Are you not well? Do you need something? I insisted, seeing that she was staggering and sweaty. Of course, a trek under the sun with that big belly, for someone who's not used to moving around, could only have exhausted her. I went to Tulù's place. How come, did you speak with him? No, I spoke with her. His new partner, Andrea? What did you say to each other? *Nonna*, it's too complicated, but anyway she slapped me and I kicked her. You are truly crazy, you knew he was with another girl, why did you go to their place? I just wanted to see Tulù's face, hear his voice and tell him I'm going to name the kid Prometheus. That's it? That's it. So why did this Andrea get angry? Well, because I jokingly said that the baby might even be Tulù's. You are so reckless. Where was Tulù? How do I know? He wasn't there, the idiot thought I wanted to blackmail her: You've come to ask money for a child you don't know whose it is? You are a wretch, what did you ask her? I didn't ask for anything, *nonna*, I just explained to her that I'm in deep shit and don't even have the money to buy myself a decent dress because mine are all too tight. So you went there to beg, you really are nuts, begging from someone you don't even know, who owes you nothing! But I wanted to talk to Tulù. As soon as she told you he wasn't there, you should have left, what does she have to do with all of this? That fucking Andrea is an idiot, she doesn't know anything about Tulù, and in my opinion she doesn't even love him. I, on the other hand, know everything about him, I know every inch of his body and of his buzzed head, and she dares to treat me like an intruder, she just got on my nerves, don't you get it? No, I don't get it at all, Lori, I think you're out of your mind.

July 30

The heat is melting my brain. Lori's belly has become a dome. She barely walks around the house, she's in her nightgown all day, doesn't wash or get dressed, more and more sulky and discontented. She's eating now, though, and at every meal she asks for fried eggs, cutlets, pasta with tomato sauce, baked fish, roasted potatoes, and she shoves down everything I cook. She has in fact gained weight and her feet are swollen. Whenever I can I consult her gynecologist, Dr. Amelia, who reassures me: the baby is fine, he'll come out big and plump, we may have to cut, but that doesn't matter, she'll not be the first nor the last to have a cesarean.

I feel more and more alone in this house inhabited by a dead woman and a live one who also seems dead. She doesn't even write in her diary anymore, the very lazy Lori. She left the key to her hiding place in the dresser drawer. I could go and take a peek, but I'm keeping my curiosity at bay. It's been a while since I've seen her bent over her little notebook with tulips on the cover.

August 2

This morning Simone gave me some olive oil rolls, fresh and still warm: For *your Maria* he said after dragging me to the back of the shop for a usual kiss. We embraced in that perfume of yeast and flour, our tongues know each other, they caress, our lips press one against the other with renewed sensuality. Even if deep down there's a desperation in our kissing: for him, trapped in a marriage whose sole purpose was to have a son with a young woman who can't seem to get pregnant, for me, trapped in a house where a daughter lies and not knowing whether she will live or not.

You know, I've thought about leaving my wife and living with you. With me? I'm crazy for our kisses. But you wouldn't if we were free to do it at any moment, and then, don't forget I have a comatose daughter at home and I can't leave her. And besides, Simone, know this: our kisses are wonderful because they are stolen, because we're in the back of the shop, and we get along because you're impotent and I'm an old woman. Yeah, I guess you're right, Gesuina, he contritely admitted, you're always the wiser one, but promise me that we will never stop kissing, I need it like I need air to breathe. The promise was sanctioned by a last kiss, so sweet and penetrating. *Give me a thousand kisses and then a hundred more / then another thousand, and then a hundred more. . . .* We embraced in the throes of a desperate, lovingly impotent solidarity.

August 18

The heat is showing no signs of letting up. It hasn't rained in months and the air is dry and stinks of burned gasoline. Lori goes around the house half-naked, slamming doors, shuffling, her hair stuck to her skull, dark circles under her eyes, shortness of breath. Only when the nurses are here does she cover up, but she normally locks herself up in her room and doesn't even greet them. Maria, with all the care from Angelo, Alessia, and me, is always clean and tidy in her bed that smells of freshly ironed linen, she sleeps blissfully, her face is truly serene, as if she were dreaming of good things.

The published book, *Madame Bovary* by Gustave Flaubert, translated by Maria Cascadei, arrived yesterday. I brought it to my daughter's bedside; I laid the book on her chest and spoke to her very softly.

Here's the book that you labored over, Maria, look at how well it came out, look at the beautiful edition they sent you! Look, on the cover is a woman with hair tied back, the well-drawn ears, the lively eyes, the beautiful rosy mouth, the blue dress the author describes when he talks about

Emma, look, these are your words that you worked so hard on. Hours and hours at your desk, next to the *Larousse* dictionary that is almost falling apart from all your consulting, and all the sheets of paper that you filled up before transcribing everything on the computer and delivering it to the editor, do you remember? you were so happy to have finished the work on time and you were waiting for the money before leaving with François who had managed to get two months off. . . . And how did he manage to get two months off? He had refused all the days off to which he was entitled, accumulated unpaid overtime and that added up to two months of freedom from the office.

I still have your letters from Holland, my dear Maria, I reread them every now and then, you spoke to us about Van Gogh, your passion, do you remember? and the strolls that you and your beloved would take along the canals and the boats you would take and the herring and the tulips. Speaking of which, I haven't watered the tulips that are suffering on the terrace, I'm afraid I've neglected them a little, but I promise you: this very evening I will water them very well. You know you are really pretty, prettier than ever my dear Maria? you've changed in these past months, you've become paler but also more serene, less wary and frowning. I hope it's not a sign of surrender. You must resist, you must resist, Maria, because we're waiting for a sign, just a blink of your eye, to breathe fully again. Everything in this house is on hold, awaiting your return, a still house, a fairy house, a haunted house, as Lori says, the house of the sleeping beauty who awaits the happy prince who will give her a kiss. I should have you listen to the theories Simone the baker has about kisses, they're somewhat ridiculous but also full of a sweet fascination. The baker Simone has herded all his sexuality into his kisses, he doesn't know what to do with intercourse, for him it's something vulgar, violent, futile: the genitals are too close to the orifices that expel excrement, urine, all the stuff that stinks, what do they have to do with love? The mouth is a different story, the mouth tastes of coffee, of sugar, of ice cream, of cinnamon, of wine, even of tobacco, how can that compare with shit? Do you remember the Neapolitan song that goes: *Ma cu sti modi oje Brigida / tazza e' cafè parite / sotto tenite o zuccaro / e 'ncoppa amara site / ma i' tanto ch'aggia vutà / tanto che aggia a girà, / che o' ddoce sotta a tazza / fin'a mmocca m'ha dda arrivà.* [But with these ways, oh Brigida / you're like a cup of coffee / you're sugar at the bottom / and you're bitterness on top / but if I swirl / and if I stir, / the sweetness at the bottom of the cup / will eventually reach my mouth.] Simone sang it to me the other day just before he glued his lips to mine. He makes me laugh, that Simone the baker, when he pronounces on such matters, but I have to tell you his kisses taste like sugar and cinnamon just like the song says, and he has such sweetness on those lips that it makes me want to say, one more kiss. . . .

It would be so nice if you would open an eyelid, Maria, and force a smile, even just barely, just a measly little smile to tell us you're still here, that you haven't left us forever. Besides, your body doesn't want to leave us forever, you know that as well, your heart continues to beat, your pulse pulsates, only your thoughts seem to have vanished, as if suspended in nothingness, but your hair still grows, your nails that I clip now and then, very carefully so as not to hurt you, they still sprout, which means you are still here, your body wants to live, Maria, it wants to get up and walk. Why don't you come down from that void and come to say good morning to us? Mr. Flaubert and all of us, including the nurses Angelo and Alessia, not to mention Lori and even Simone the baker, we are all waiting for you to give a nod, a single nod, even a sigh, and we will dance with joy.

2:OO P.M.

When Angelo arrived with his ship in motion on his tense muscles, he asked me what a book was doing on the chest of the inpatient, that's the term he used, in his hospital jargon. He threw the book on the small sofa that's tucked under the window and began to work on Maria's inert body. The wounds have healed, did you see? He speaks to me with arrogance, as if to demonstrate that he knows what he's doing, that his care is necessary and it's useless for me to remind him that it was nothing short of brazen to have sex with the nurse Alessia next to the comatose Maria.

The thing is that I never reproached him at all, but he thinks that I want to and that he's preventing me from doing so with his cocky and provocative attitude. I think this one, sooner or later, will wake up, he pronounced as he massaged her feet and bent her knees to keep the muscles awake, as he often says. I concentrated on his ship that, as Angelo shook his arms, unfurled its sails, and I glanced at the mermaid who keeps stretching out her small head with long green tresses toward her beloved who is locked away in that vessel of yesteryear. They will never meet and yet love from afar never ceases to torment them.

Meanwhile the owner of those arms kept on talking: he told me his wife reads and asked if I would lend him a book given that there are so many in this house. I agreed. Besides, *signora* Maria will no longer read them, he added, but then he corrected himself, even if she were to come back to life, I don't think she'll feel like reading, with all her sore muscles, even eyes have muscles, you know? I nodded and he continued undaunted telling me his wife has diabetes, and as a result lost her job, and he has to work twice as hard to bring money home. He added that he has four children, all little, and he can barely feed them. All this to justify a foolish act by a licensed nurse? Okay, okay, just shut up, I would have liked to tell him, but I let him vent, I knew he needed to. I don't know if my tolerance stems from generosity or if it's only a tactic to keep him as a friend, or worse yet a gesture of vile consent: the fear of losing his care of Maria's body which she so desperately needs. I understood that he would like some extra money and I'll do whatever I can to get it for him even if we're tightening our belts here and skimping even on milk to make ends meet just with my injections.

August 24

Lori has breakdowns. She locks herself up in her room and cries while listening to Hindi songs from records Tulù had given to her. I should grab her by the arm and drag her outside of this house frozen in time and cursed by the gods, but I can't leave Maria alone. I no longer even trust the nurses. I now try to be here every time they come to take care of her.

When I'm alone with her, I've taken up the habit of reading to her a few pages from *Madame Bovary* in the translation which she spent almost a year completing. An accurate translation and very pleasing in the choice of words, as I notice when reading it aloud. She lies there motionless and ashen, but at times I have the impression that something in the sound of the words gets through to her brain, passing as steamy water through her closed ears.

In reading about Charles, who walks into the classroom and who, after observing his classmates toss their caps onto their desks without missing, in turn throws his cap which ends up under the teacher's desk gliding along the entire length of the classroom floor, I started to laugh to myself. And for a moment I had the impression that Maria's body shook, a little subterranean laugh that made her eyelids quiver and her belly jerk. I looked at her, holding my breath, but she was motionless as always. I went back to reading and laughing, but then I simply couldn't contain myself. I got up, ran to knock on Lori's door to tell her that Maria had laughed with me. It was probably just my impression, but the bed did shake for a moment, I was sure of it, and I wanted Lori to know. I found her lying down with two pillows under her head, and a book in her hand. Oh, you've finally started reading again, I said. She smiled at me. Something unheard of. She didn't chase me from her room, she didn't let out an angry grunt, she just smiled at me. Is mom coming back to us? she asked softly, almost as if it were obvious, a matter of minutes. I certainly hope so; the doctor says it's possible even if not guaranteed.

September 10

The baby is born. Premature, but very healthy. For once I left Maria in the hands of the nurse with tattooed arms and I went with Lori to the hospital where she had a delivery that was much easier than expected. There was no need for a cesarean section. Dr. Amelia came by to greet the new mother. The attending doctor, Dr. DeAngelis, flashed me a big smile as he hurried down the corridor, sliding along in his white plastic clogs. Little Prometheus immediately screamed out his desire to live, showing off his ample and powerful lungs. Lori is recovering quickly. And she's already wondering if she can return to school and how to handle the nursing. The childbirth has visibly changed her: no more grimaces, weeping, anger, and grumpiness, but a peaceful desire to keep the little body of her newborn son attached to her. She doesn't want to let go of him even for a moment and she's happy she has plenty of milk and the greedy baby is ever ready to latch on to her nipple.

A Madonna with child on her lap, Alessia commented on watching Lori who quickly returned home. Alessia comes by two days in a row, substituting for Angelo who was forced to stay home because of a high fever. This absence seemed strange to me, almost as if the alternation of day and night were distorted. And I realized that, with my mind's eye, I was looking for the ship with the unfurled sails on Angelo's left arm, while on his right arm I was stalking the woman with the green tresses and fishtail who was in love with the unseen sailor. Lori raises a flag when she has to breastfeed. If she could, she would do it out on the balcony, inviting all the passersby to admire her turgid breast to which her child clings, a child with thighs so fat they are reminiscent of certain little angels flying around the altars of baroque churches, all curls and pudgy arms topped with two dragonfly wings. The newborn child already has a full head of thick hair, eyes of an intense blue almost black, flecked with tiny gold flakes.

Shall I phone François to let him know of his son's birth? I asked Lori, but she forbade me. The baby is mine and he has nothing to do with it. But he's his father, I insisted. Has he ever shown any regard for me or the little one? Let him stay in his Lille, I don't want to see him. Meanwhile the new mom eats a pound of ricotta a day, then prosciutto and cooked ham, cutlets, roast chicken, *the blackberry tart that you make so well, nonna*. But I don't have time for tarts. My days are strictly divided into precise tasks: groceries, injections that I now charge more for, especially if I have to make house calls; if they come to me, I charge less because that means I don't waste time on buses and the subway. Then there's cooking, reading Flaubert at Maria's bedside, caring for the baby when his mother is resting exhausted by a slumber continually interrupted by nighttime feedings. Prometheus almost never cries, he's always hungry and when he wants his mother's breast to suckle, he lets out these inhuman screams. Lori gets up five, six times a night to feed him but he's never satisfied, he'd like to stay there, stuck to his mother's nipple.

September 25

Dear Diary,

I've totally neglected you, but I was feeling so bad, so bad that I wanted to die, in this house that *nonna* says is under a spell, with mom who I want to think is sleeping and not that she's slipping away, but how much does this wise mother sleep, to the point that she never wakes up even when the sweet smell of coffee permeates the house? the pregnancy was tough, I hated this child that made me suffer, I first detested the cold of January and February and then the heat of July and August that invaded every room like an enraged beast, I thought I would've spit this child out and be done with it, I wouldn't have given it a second thought, I would've entrusted it to *nonna* and taken off on a long trip, I didn't want to hear about this haunted house anymore, about the whale body I had made of myself, of a head empty of thoughts and words, if I had a bit more courage I'd have thrown myself from the fourth floor, but since I'm lazy, I put it all off and it was my salvation because after Prometheus was born everything changed, the spell was broken, even mom apparently started to laugh in listening to the story of little Charles Bovary who threw his cap on his desk, missing it and making it slide across the classroom floor, I don't know

whether *nonna* imagined the whole thing when she swears
mom started to laugh, she seems to me to be the same
Maria of a year ago, cleaned and perfumed but lying
motionless on her bed like an embalmed corpse, I looked
at her for a long time, but I don't think there's anything
new, she just seems a little more pale, she's as beautiful as
a statue, she reminds me of a saint enclosed in a casket,
poor mom, what have they done to you? and why don't you
decide to just go away if you don't want to stay with us
anymore? meanwhile, *nonna* reads passages from *Madame
Bovary* aloud to you, in your wonderful translation, and
by the way there's been a review published that speaks
enthusiastically of the Italian version by Maria Cascadei,
too bad you can't read it, you would be happy, after so
much work and effort that the poor *Larousse* now touts
tattered pages, the tulips you brought from Holland have
all blossomed at the same time and are beautiful, it's like
they're made of ceramic, as you said, some are vibrant red,
some yellow as egg yolk and still others of a lilac that
recalls butterfly wings, they've raised their heads and are
standing upright on the balcony as if to say life is good,
but is life good? ever since my son was born, the tulips
make me happy and I think yes, life is good: *life is good* as
the TV says as soon as I turn it on, and it seems that
everything in this house is turning on, except for mom's
eyes that remain mysteriously closed, *life is good* to me and
my son, Prometheus, and it probably is for *nonna* too, who
from an unflagging actress and flirty little butterfly has
transformed into a formidable and tireless governess who
plans everything and faces everything with the courage of
a lioness? *Nonna* Gesuina even took a correspondence
course in nursing, and now, in addition to shots in the
butt, she sets up intravenous drips, treats bedsores, takes

blood pressure, medicates burns, in short, she is a paid home nurse and earns enough for the two of us, actually the three of us, because Prometheus eats at full blast and so do I.

October 5

The countryside is burning. The woods on the hill are burning. The city is threatened by the fire. Many houses on the hillock have been evacuated and soon will be devoured by the flames. They say it's all arson, but how is it possible that a person of sound mind starts a fire knowing it will devour not only trees and precious plants, but will burn many animals alive, large and small, it will raise intoxicating smoke, it will reduce plants, flowers, houses, and human beings to ashes? A black, greasy vapor has even entered our house from the open windows. At night you can see the hill overlooking the city, crested by red-and-yellow fires. And the smoke envelops the city, suffocating it, poisoning its air.

They caught three boys who doused a poor cat with gasoline and threw it into some dry plants, thus unwittingly spreading the fire throughout the woods. They asked them why they did it and they answered: For fun. Is that what goes on in a pyromaniac's head? I have a mind to take them one by one and bring them near the fires, forcing them to put out those flames, to take out from the ashes the cadavers of the dead animals to bury them while breathing in the fumes that plague the city: would it serve any purpose? I doubt it, but I want to hope so, my faith in the power of reason sustains me. My granddaughter, Lori, seems to have been reborn, along with her baby. She's again taken up writing in her quad-ruled notebook with tulips on the cover, she goes out every morning with her son in her arms, she takes him to the public gardens, she holds him tightly as they go down the slide, she places him in the swing and pushes him higher and higher. You're crazy to treat a newborn as if he were four years old! But she just laughs and says that her son isn't an ordinary baby, he's a marvel, a little Hercules who clings to the ropes with his little hands that have just come out of his mother's womb and lunges forward, shaking his thick and sturdy little legs. These days, though, we're all closed up in the house because of the smoke that makes us cough and tear up. Let's hope the fire doesn't come to town.

I continue to read passages from *Madame Bovary* to Maria, the Sleeping Beauty. Look, Maria, the woods are burning. You have to wake up, we have to leave this inertia, we have to open our eyes, your life depends on it. But she seems not to hear my words, nor to smell the smoke that makes us cough, nor to feel the heat of the flames that engulf the outskirts of the city.

December 10

The days have gotten shorter and the sun has grown weak, almost extinguished. Luckily, with the first rains the woods stopped burning. Many in the area have come down with a new influenza, which has been dubbed the Hungarian flu since it started there, and they're calling me for shots. I raised my fees but they haven't protested. There are four of us here now and I'm the only one earning anything. I run around all day long. I had to give up on my heels and buy myself a pair of flat, comfortable shoes. Lori says I look like a duck when I walk fast in those alpine shoes. I decided to buy myself a moped like the one Lori has so I can get around faster. She laughs, she thinks I'll look ridiculous on that contraption at my age. You could find a small job to do at home, I tell her sternly. But then I have to admit that it would be hard to work with that little devil of a son of hers who eats like an ogre and is becoming bigger and bigger and more demanding even if he doesn't cry; he understands perfectly well that there's someone in the house who is sleeping and he mustn't disturb her. When placed on the carpet, he seems like he's ready to crawl, and he puts everything he finds in his mouth.

The other day Prometheus put the heel of a shoe his mother had given him in his mouth and he was sucking on it as if it were a licorice stick. I snatched it from his hands, but in doing so, I almost fell flat on the floor, such was the strength he was using to keep that shoe tight to his chest. When I scold him, he lies down belly up like a dog and starts to laugh kicking his bare feet in the air. He's a strong-willed child, but he knows the art of pleasing. He has seduced all the folks in the neighborhood, even the baker Simone who, as soon as he saw him, propped him up in between two round freshly baked loaves of bread, placed a chocolate cookie in his fingers and did not forgo pulling me off to the back room for a kiss, gluing his beautiful cinnamon-flavored mouth to mine. A hasty embrace because I was afraid Prometheus would fall from the chair along with his cookie. But fortunately, nothing happened: he was happily waiting for me, gnawing on his chocolate cookie.

I grabbed the bread and went home. I found Lori in the kitchen hugging Angelo. I noticed the heap of muscles that raised the ship's sails on his left arm and the mermaid raising her head on his right arm. They straightened up, pretending nothing had happened. Nor did I reproach them. Only later, when Angelo had left, did I remind Lori that the man was married, with four kids, and besides, he had already had sex with Nurse Alessia. She laughed: I know, *nonna*, we were just experimenting. Experimenting what? Happy coexistence: we've been seeing each other for months and he told me he gets excited when he sees me, and I get excited too when I see his tanned neck, I like that ship that moves its sails on his arm and his smile enchants me. But he never smiles! Maybe not for you, but he smiles for me, a lot too.

Are you forgetting he's married with four small children? I insisted on calling her to accountability, Look who's talking, *nonna*, you who for quite a while have been seeing that darn baker who's married to a bespectacled corpse, even if he doesn't have any kids, but he's married and what are you doing behaving like the adulteress Emma Bovary? She takes on a defiant air when she says these things and I can't even say she's wrong: we both are seeing married men even if hers passes from kisses to intercourse, while mine sticks to kisses and philosophies on life. Think of your mother whom you forced into this state of inertia by your recklessness, and try to help out more at home, I can't take care of everything! At that moment we heard a thud and Lori ran to see what had happened: Prometheus had fallen, or rather he had thrown himself from the bed and was crawling on the floor.

December 30

Today something extraordinary happened. Maria opened her eyes and looked at me without seeing but as if asking herself where she was. I've never seen such bright and at the same time blind pupils. She looked around and winced in pain. Maria! I screamed, jumping from the chair. I was reading a

Baudelaire poem to her: *Under a dim light / Runs, dances and twists for no reason / Life, brazen and garish.* A poem that she liked very much. But immediately afterward she closed her eyes again and returned to her absent state. For a few seconds her fingers drummed on the linen as if playing an imaginary piano. Lori, come see, Lori, hurry!

Lori came in still in her pajamas and scolded me: You're seeing things, *nonna*, mom will never wake up again and when Prometheus turns three we'll all bury her together in the cemetery outside the city. Why are you saying that, Lori? I believe your mother is slowly climbing up the steep rocks of awakening, she hears us and understands everything and soon she will start walking again like you and me. She laughed: *Nonna*, you are a unrelenting romantic, in fact I'll go so far as to say that as you've gotten older you're moving away from the nice, understanding grandmother I used to know and becoming more like my mother, Maria, in character, dreams and desires, but honestly I preferred you as you were before, you're getting old, *nonna*, I wouldn't want you to up and die leaving me alone with my comatose mother and a son who wreaks havoc, what would I do without you?

I didn't understand whether it was a declaration of affection or a confession of weakness. Lori doesn't know what it is to work: before, her mother supported her with her translations, now it's me with injections: what would she do on her own? The fact is, Lori, that I have no intention of dying before my time! I said sweetly, and she started to laugh as did I, and even the baby, infected by our happiness, opened wide his little toothless mouth kicking his little feet in the air.

At that moment we heard a little laughter coming from Maria's bed and we turned around to see. Maria had her eyes closed but a slight, halting laugh was drawn on her parted lips, accompanied by a throaty gurgle. It was really true: she was laughing, my Maria, and I knelt down next to her, took her hand and kissed it as tears ran down my cheeks. Lori, with the baby in her arms, stood there stock-still, incapable of saying a single word. She too was crying, and the baby began, with a kid-like gesture, to lick her tears. Even those are good to eat, I said, and we all started laughing again but from happiness.

Notes on Contributors

DACIA MARAINI is the most prominent living Italian woman writer today and one of the most studied living Italian writers. Her prolific work of over fifty years, which has been recognized by numerous awards and prizes, embraces many literary genres, including historical fictional narrative, the short story, theater, poetry, and journalism. Her formation as humanist and journalist echoes throughout her works, bringing to the public consciousness major issues of women's rights, both through a historical lens (Mary Stuart, Isabella di Morra, Catarina da Siena) and with reference to current events including human trafficking of children, victimization, and the wave of "femicide" that has spread through Italy in recent years. She succeeds in raising public awareness through the powerful, accessible, well-chosen word as career novelist, playwright, and op-ed essayist for Italy's major national newspapers. Writing is her vocation and occupation. Widely translated in over twenty-four languages, sometimes inter-semiotically through major motion pictures, her voice is heard around the world.

Maraini has been recognized with the Campiello and Strega Prizes, the most prestigious literary awards in Italy. She is frequently called on to serve on juries for similar literary prizes, especially those that reward new and upcoming writers. She fosters the love of reading and writing by her visits to elementary, middle, and high schools in Italy, as well as offering talks and master classes as distinguished international visiting scholar at major colleges and universities internationally. Moreover, Maraini was awarded an honoris causa degree by two U.S. universities (Middlebury College in Vermont and John Cabot University in Rome) and three Italian universities (University of the Studies of Foggia, University of Macerata, and University L'Orientale of Naples).

ELVIRA G. DI FABIO holds a PhD from Harvard University, Department of Romance Languages and Literatures (RLL), with a doctoral dissertation on the phonomorphology of the Italian verb system. She coordinated the Italian language program at Harvard from 1990 until 2020 and served as RLL's director of language programs from 2016 to 2020. She taught Italian from beginning to advanced, as well as special content courses including translation courses from Italian to English (Italian 50 Literary Translation). In her course on Romance translation: theory and practice (Romance Studies 101), students worked on texts in one of the four major Romance languages of their choice. Classroom discussions centered on comparing translations and finding common issues among the languages and their transfer to English.

Di Fabio first met Dacia Maraini in 1997 when the author was invited to Harvard as a visiting scholar. Di Fabio has since been privileged to follow Maraini's public life as well as invite her back to Harvard on several occasions for guest lectures and writing workshops. Di Fabio also considers herself privileged to share Maraini's love for the Abruzzo region of Italy where they both have homes as retreats—Dacia in the mountainous woodlands of the Aquila province and Elvira in those of the Pescara province. Maraini's admiration, awe, and care of the natural setting and its four-footed inhabitants, the unchartered mountain forests, the spirituality of these fairly untrodden paths are convincing evidence of the depth of Maraini's sentiments and the honesty of her work.

Di Fabio most recently contributed translated selections of Maraini's works to *Writing like Breathing. An Homage to Dacia Maraini*. The series, compiled and edited by Michelangelo La Luna, is divided into five major volumes, representing the rich spectrum of Maraini's works from 1962 to the present: I. Autobiography, novels, short stories, and poems; II. Plays; III. Articles; IV. Essays, talks, and interviews; V. Festschrift. Di Fabio contributed to the first and second volumes, a translation task that afforded her a microscopic appreciation of Maraini's effective choice of words and syntax.

SARA TEARDO is a senior lecturer at the Department of French and Italian at Princeton University and holds a PhD in Italian Studies and a MAT in Spanish from Rutgers University. She has published on Italian women writers and translation. In collaboration with Princeton colleague Susan Stewart, she edited and translated Laudomia Bonanni's posthumous novel *The Reprisal*.